D1120026

The House of Medici

The House of Medici

Seeds of Decline

A Novel

Edward Charles

Skyhorse Publishing

CONTENTS

Florence
May 1481

"Heaven has no rage like love to hatred turned
Nor hell a fury like a woman scorned"

- William Congreve *The Mourning Bride"* 1697

Chapter 1
An Independent Monk

For years they had taken comfort in knowing that the city of Florence was well-protected. Lying in a broad valley-basin, it was surrounded to the north and the south by great curves of hills and mountains.

The road northward, from Bologna, was protected by the Mugello, traditional Medici country – a region they always considered a place of safety.

But the land to the south was different. Quite different. And as the party made its way over the hills south of the city, along the road that would eventually pass to the west of Siena before continuing onward, towards the distant *Colline Metallifere*, they knew they were approaching new, unwelcoming territory. Here they would never feel entirely safe. Siena was the sworn enemy of Florence and ever since leaving Colle di Val D'Elsa early that morning they had known themselves to be deep in the Colle Senese – enemy country.

However, as any member of a banking family knows, there are no certainties in this life, and when you are unwell, and when the cure lies beyond unsafe places, sometimes you simply have to draw a deep breath, take a chance, trust in God, and go.

For too long now there had been war, and an uncomfortably nearby war at that. As they looked around they were aware that less than three years earlier papal troops had attacked the Val de Chiana, only a few miles to their left. Then, a year later, the Duke of Calabria had routed Florentine troops at Poggio Imperiale, driving the Florentines back to San Casciano only eight miles from the southern gates of the city itself. And less than eighteen months previously, in November, the enemies of Florence had laid siege to Colle di Val D'Elsa itself and subdued it.

These were not good times to be riding alone. And that is why they were accompanied by servants and ten heavily-armed soldiers, all in Lorenzo's livery.

Despite being in enemy territory, or perhaps because of it, they had been making good time. They had left the city of Florence four days earlier, in the afternoon, through the *Porta Romana* and by the first evening, with the great hills still ahead of them, had decided to stop at San Casciano. The following morning had been hard work, climbing and climbing until, for the first time, at Fabbrica, they had been able to rest and get their breath back. Then along the ridge road, through Passignano until at Tavarnelle they were able to look further south, over the edge, down, leftward into Chianti and to their right into the Val d'Elsa.

After all that effort, the third day had been a pleasure. The air was clear, the road good and downhill all the way, along the river at Poggibonsi and into safe hands at Colle di Val D'Elsa. As expected, *La Magnifica* had to pay the price of hospitality. A Medici wife and mother could not pass through this valley without making a donation to the Church of Santa Maria Della Spugna and blessing the waters of the Gora, the great fast-flowing canal that powered the paper mills along its banks.

So the formalities had been maintained. At a dinner in her honour, Johannes de Medemblick presented her with a bound copy of *De Materia Medica*, a translation of Pedacius Dioscorides' ancient work translated by Peter of Albano – a volume which he himself had printed in Colle only three years previously. It had been a proud moment for him, made especially surprising to many present when Mona Lucrezia admitted that, had the occasion arisen, she would have been more than able to read the great work in its original Greek.

Now it was the fourth day of their journey and as the sun grew stronger over to their left, they began climbing once again, south-west now, out onto the Piano de Val D'Elsa, a small plain of rich cornfields, waving gently in the breeze. Ahead of them, standing proud on its hilltop, was Càsole d'Elsa, their next destination. It was already warm. Very warm, and by the time they reached that faraway hill, they knew it would be hot. Already the air above the hillside ahead of them was beginning to shimmer in the summer heat.

Lucrezia Tornabuoni de Medici slapped the back of her neck

with the palm of her left hand. 'Why are black cattle flies the most irritating? Is it because they are more stupid than the others, or are they, in truth, intelligent and for reasons known only to them, more persistent in their attentions?'

Piero Malagonelle turned to Giovanni di Pace and grinned. It was typical of her opening remarks, designed perhaps to put them on their toes and to initiate an hour of rhetoric. They knew there was nothing she liked better, and they both knew that, however hard they tried, they wouldn't win. She would never stop until she had beaten them. Nevertheless, their conversation would keep them entertained, as it had each day of their journey, so far.

How to respond? That was the first question. She had, as they knew well, a mind like a lawyer and, like a lawyer, she never misused or wasted a word. So what now? Was this to be a debate about cattle flies of varying colours? Was it specifically the black ones they were debating? Or were they to accept as a fact the assertion that it was the black cattle flies that could be relied upon to trouble them most, and concentrate the debate purely on the reasons why?

Careful not to charge-in and be wrong-footed (he had been caught that way too often in the past), Piero replied to her question with a question of his own. 'Is it one *specific* fly that is troubling you this morning, Mona Lucrezia, or are we about to declare war on *all* cattle flies?' He winked at Giovanni as he answered, telling him that it was his turn next. Perhaps if they ganged up on her they may win once, before they reached Càsole.

But her reply surprised them both. 'One, of course. That one.'

Now, for the first time, she indicated with a stab of her thumb over her shoulder. 'The man in black, trailing behind us. He has been hovering there, half a mile back, ever since we left Colli. And, furthermore, I am sure I saw him yesterday also. I think he's following us. And now he's starting to get on my nerves.'

The smile already gone from his face, Piero clicked his fingers. But already the captain of their armed guard was responding. He turned and, shading his eyes with his right hand, looked back.

11

'You mean the young monk? Yes he's been shadowing us for a couple of days, since Tavarnelle. I decided he was harmless, a lone monk, on foot and carrying a heavy bag over his shoulder. I thought perhaps he was nervous walking alone and felt safer hanging onto our coat-tails. But if he's an irritant, *Madonna*, I'll bring him in and we can question him.'

Lucrezia shrugged, but they both knew she would not let go of things that easily. Already Benvisto could see that she was irritated by the fact that he, captain of her guard, had noticed the man and said and done nothing. With hindsight it had been a mistake. She was good at delegating work, but she did like to make the decisions herself.

'You four. Come with me,' he commanded.

Together, four of the armed guard turned and set off behind their captain. The others stopped their horses, turned, leaned on their saddle pommels, and watched. Behind them their three carts were toiling along, the un-mounted servants walking easily, their packs thrown into the carts. And beyond them, just where the land started to flatten off, the monk kept walking towards them.

It didn't take long. The man made no attempt to escape. In fact he seemed almost pleased to be recognized. He raised a hand in welcome as the soldiers surrounded him, then, without apparent demur, swung his bag onto the other shoulder and started to return with them.

Lucrezia shaded her eyes. Benvisto's eyes must be good. She could not have told that the monk was young. In fact, she hadn't even recognized that he was a monk at all. Just a lone walker, in black, and covered in their dust. But then she would be fifty-five next birthday and the young soldier couldn't be more than twenty-three. Oh to be that young again.

The soldiers returned. And with them, walking as fast as he could, came the monk. He stood, threw back his cowl, and looked up at her. His face was unattractive, the dark grey eyes small and, although intelligent, resentful, whilst his nose was huge and either hooked or roughly broken. His lips were thick, like an eel's. Yet for all the charmless qualities of his face, despite having been brought to her by an armed guard, and standing alone on a dirt path surrounded by horses, the young man seemed to radiate confidence and self-knowledge.

'Have you been following us?' she asked.

He looked straight up at Lucrezia, level-eyed and without any sign of deference. 'Yes. Since Tavarnelle.' His look was not angry, or even disrespectful.

Immediately, he had her full attention. 'Why is that? You know who I am?'

'Of course. You are Madonna Lucrezia Tornabuoni de Medici, wife of the late Piero de Medici and mother of the Magnificent Lorenzo. You are on your way to Bagno à Morba, to seek the cure.'

'You are well-informed. But you sound as if you do not think the Bagno will improve my condition. Do you not have faith in such things?'

'I put no faith in things, in places or in objects. My faith is in God. As for the Bagno, I see no reason why it should do you harm, but if, as I suspect, your discomforts are sent by God as a punishment for your sins, then no amount of bathing in mineral-rich water will wash them away. Only confession of your sins and true redemption will do that.'

Lucrezia raised an eyebrow, and then flicked her eyes from one companion to the other, surprised and not a little amused. 'You seem very confident in your views.'

The young monk nodded and smiled. Just slightly, But he didn't say anything else.

'What is your name?'

'My name is Girolamo Savonarola. I am a monk, until recently the teaching Master of Novices, at the Monastery of Santa Maria dei Angeli, in Ferrara. Before that, I was at San Domenico in Bologna.'

Lucrezia frowned, as if something was wrong, and then wrinkled her nose. 'Your accent is not from Bologna.'

'I was born and first educated in Ferrara.'

Again the frown. 'You have walked here from Ferrara?'

'Of course. I walk everywhere. It is part of my penance. I

walked first to Florence, but when they told me you had left there, I followed.'

'And why do you presume to follow me?' Having overcome her initial suspicions, Mona Lucrezia seemed entertained by his manner. Now her voice was becoming clipped and combative.

'I have reason to speak to you, Madonna. Privately. In confidence. To do so in Florence was clearly impossible, so when I heard that you planned to spend a month at the Bagno, I decided to follow you, and to approach you at an appropriate time.'

'And what time would you have deemed "appropriate"?'

'At any time which was convenient to you and when you were not busy with other things. I need time. Time to talk to you properly, about a subject of importance to me. The Bagno seemed an admirable opportunity.'

Benvisto nudged his horse forward, perhaps believing that the monk's directness was disrespectful. 'Do you want me to send him packing?' Unperturbed, the monk leaned back to avoid the horse's head and took two paces backward. But then he continued to stand, still looking at Lucrezia, and waiting for her response.

Lucrezia shook her head. 'No. The monk answers truly and directly. I cannot punish him for that.' She kept her eyes on Savonarola, who remained unmoved, his leather bag still over one shoulder. 'Join us. We shall feed and house you, as befits a Dominican. Your mission intrigues me and your presumption is right. I shall, indeed, have considerable time while I am at the Bagno.'

As she said it, she noticed the look of surprise on her companions' faces and grinned to herself. 'Once I have discharged my managerial responsibilities.' She smiled as she said it and turned her head. 'You may not have been aware that I not only visit the baths, but I own them, and with my project manager, Ser Piero Malagonelle here, I am redeveloping them. Meanwhile, Ser Giovanni di Pace,' she pointed to him as she spoke, 'manages the business on a day-to-day basis, on my behalf.'

Savonarola shook his head. 'I didn't know.'

'Nevertheless, I shall have leisure a-plenty, I am sure.' Lucrezia turned her horse. 'We shall speak later.'

She kicked her horse forward, toward Càsole d'Elsa, the rich orange of its stonework standing out high above and ahead of them. Behind her, the monk fell into place, the bag still heavy over his shoulder.

Chapter 2
A Confessional Arrangement

'You sent for me, Mona Lucrezia?' Savonarola's face was bright and alert; as if he had been up for hours.

Which, in reality, he had.

~

CÀSOLE D'ELSA
Dawn, 15th May 1481

He wakes and he sees the sun rise. Not a difficult thing to do when you have slept fitfully on a bare roof in a Tuscan hill-town, with a leather bag containing a bible, a breviary and the only clean shirt you own as your only pillow.

His first action, as always, is to strip naked and wash the bloodstains from around his waist, where the spiked metal belt reminds him of his sins. He washes the belt carefully and does the same with his hair shirt. It's another daily reminder of the imperfections of life, including his own. Then he puts the belt back on, together with his alternative hair shirt, followed by the comfortingly harsh material of his black cassock.

He's ready for her.

Daily penance, he believes, is an essential way of life. But he also believes that cleanliness is close to godliness, if only because it is essential for survival. If he is to make a mark on the world, he cannot afford to let his wounds become infected. Practicality is as essential as fervour if you are to achieve anything.

As the first sunlight pierces the valley, he walks down the hill and into the fields. The choice of direction is an easy one, Càsole d'Elsa is a hilltop town, completely surrounded by fertile fields. All roads and paths from its gateways lead downward.

He turns left at the bottom of the hill, walks for one hour as he does every morning, today following the curve of the hillside and making a slow circuit of the town and its surrounding farmland. Then he returns to drink water and to eat plain bread and two pieces of fruit.

Revived, he gives thanks to God. His persistence has paid off. His opportunity has come. Now he is prepared; ready for anything the Medici woman can throw at him.

~

Lucrezia turned away from the window from where she had been studying the intricate way they drained this high plateau, and faced the young monk. She was pleased to see him again. She liked the fact that he was intelligent, and direct, and spoke plainly. Already they were making good progress.

The previous night had been busy. After praying in the great church of San Niccolò, and as always, meeting local dignitaries in the Palazzo dei Priori, she had interviewed the young priest for the first time, here in her room in the Castello of Càsole d'Elsa. It had been an interesting conversation.

~

CASTELLO, CÀSOLE D'ELSA
14th May 1481

'You said you wished to speak to me.' She wastes no time with preliminaries, as she never does, if she can avoid it.
He nods, but irritatingly, does not reply.
'Of what matter?'
He answers succinctly. 'I told you that I originated in Ferrara and am a Dominican monk. Recently I have been sent from Ferrara to Florence, to live in the Dominican Convent of San Marco. There, I shall be acting as Chief Instructor in Theology and Lecturer on Scripture.'
Lucrezia inclines her head, giving due respect. 'Congratulations. You must be a man of great learning and intellect?'
He lets that pass. 'I consider the appointment, like all appointments, to be a responsibility not an accolade. But in accordance with the Rule of our Order, I am also required to go out into the streets and to preach the gospel. It is the burden of that latter responsibility that brings me to you.'
She frowns, not following. 'How can I help you with that?'

'It has become immediately clear to me that Florence is not as other cities. At least, not like those of my acquaintance.'

'No?' She raises one eyebrow, leading him on, interested already to discover how his mind works, but maintaining her distance until she knows exactly what he wants of her.

'No. In Ferrara, where I was born and educated, the Este family and their court dominate everything. The people, perhaps for this reason, are acquiescent and passive. They take no interest in politics. But Florence appears to be completely different. Everybody there, every lord, every merchant, every goldsmith and even every shoemaker, seems to have a view on how the city should be run.'

She nods. *That's perceptive. How long has he been in the city?*

'There are other differences. Compared with Ferrara and Bologna, Florence seems to be more complicated, more sophisticated, more subtle. And the people are such negotiators, fast talkers, manipulative and clever with words. Already I see there is a huge disparity between the apparent and the real. And it is the real that I seek to understand.'

She smiles at that, the words to her mind being a compliment. 'Your observation is accurate. But I cannot change those facts. The Florence you find is the Florence you will have to deal with.' She flicks her eyes at the young monk, teasing him and measuring him in the process. 'We don't do simple. It's not...' She taps her teeth with the back of a fingernail. 'It's not stimulating enough.'

But if she hopes to upset his equilibrium with her taunts, she is disappointed.

He lets her jibes slide over him and goes straight to the point. 'Indeed. So I understand. So much is clear from the architecture and from the art. Especially the sculptures. But in order to preach the gospel to your city, I need to understand how it thinks, and if I am to do that, I need someone who truly understands the city's intricacies, someone who is able to explain to me the difference between the portrayed image and the reality beneath.'

She lifts her head tall, absorbing the compliment. 'And you think I can do that?'

'I believe no-one can do it better. That's why I pursued you.'

~

Remembering the previous evening, Lucrezia smiled to herself. It had been that phrase, that brazen, self-confident admission of purpose, that had committed her attention and made her begin to take this earnest young man more seriously.

Accepting his sincerity, she had not wasted his time by being coy, by responding with false modesty. Instead she had let the remark pass as a statement accepted for what it was worth, and immediately she had probed him further.

~

CASTELLO, CÀSOLE D'ELSA
14th May 1481

'Why should I explain Florentine reality to you? I assume this is not to be an act of charity so, as they will say to you in the Mercato Vecchio, what's in it for me?' Perhaps surprised by her directness, the young monk's grey eyes open wide. She lets him stare for a minute before explaining. 'We have already established what I can do for you.' She lifts her eyes, almost flirtatiously. 'The question now is what, if anything, can you do for me in return?'

To her surprise and without batting an eyelid, he replies immediately. 'I can save your soul.' He looks back at her with a deep intensity that matches her own.

Caught on the back foot, she feels a strong need to swallow and knows she must not. That one look tells her that he has known from the beginning what she will ask him, has already thought about his reply and has prepared himself. *He's prepared himself well.* But more than that. The expression on his face says something else. *This monk actually believes he can do it.* She lets him wait. *Inappropriate to decide too quickly. He'll read it as a sign of weakness.* Then she nods. Once. 'It's a good offer. I shall think about it. Come and see me in the morning, one hour before Terce.'

And he, similarly, shows no emotion; just nods in reply, turns away and walks out of the door.

As soon as he had left the room she had taken her usual precautions. She sent for Benvisto and asked him how safe they would be for the rest of their journey if she asked him to return immediately to Florence. And when he had given her the assurances she expected, she gave him a task.

'Return to Florence and ask my notary to undertake an urgent character check on this young priest. Tell him to send at once to Bologna and to Ferrara and to ask his contacts there what they can find out about him. I need to know how much, if at all, I can trust him.'

Benvisto, ever-reliable, was gone before dawn.

The following morning, exactly on time, the young monk was back again. Lucrezia had already made up her mind.

She had known for some time that this journey was going to be incomplete. It was three years since she had bought the Bagno à Morba, three years in which she had spent a great deal of money, all of it her own, rebuilding the springs and the wells, damming and re-routing streams, re-lining the channels, installing new settling tanks and cisterns, building the douches and the showers, the sweating rooms and the lolling pools.

She had built separate facilities for those women who did not like men ogling them whenever they took to the baths (while they, as always, strutted their own nakedness as if no one had ever stood them before a mirror and informed them of harsh reality). And she had built a guesthouse and a hotel, both again with separate, dedicated facilities for women.

The project, even by her stringent standards, had been a success. The business was thriving and yes, she still had enough faith in the waters to submit herself to their effects for a month. But curing her indigestion and relieving her eczema and her rheumatism were no longer enough. For some months now she had known with a clarity she was still careful to hide from the rest of the family that she did not have long to live.

One year? Perhaps if she was lucky, two years. Or if she was unlucky, three years, with the third providing a long and painful ending. The lumps were growing bigger and however long she soaked herself in the waters of the Bagno, she knew nothing would ever wash them away. So increasingly her body was no longer her greatest concern. Nowadays, it was her soul that needed attention. And in that matter she knew there was not too much time left.

Although he could not know it, the young monk's timing was impeccable. She had been addressing the subject privately, inside her head, for months, without guidance or solution. And now this man had, without hesitation, promised an answer. And the more she thought about it, the more she saw the sense of it. She saw it as a matter of organization.

To Lucrezia, God was part of the natural order of things, sitting at the very top of the essential hierarchy without which the world would collapse into chaos, into the anarchy of Dante's *Inferno*. It was a hierarchy of order and control. A natural hierarchy, of kings and princes and nobles and gentlemen and at the bottom, the rest – the *popolani*. A natural hierarchy of saints and popes and cardinals and bishops and common priests. A natural hierarchy that the nobility, her family and (by acceptance if not by birth) the Medici, were an important part of. A hierarchy in which she herself had a position, and an elevated position at that.

Lucrezia did not fear God. Fear of God was for the unlearned masses – the best way to keep them all in order and, besides, it gave the priests something to do. She believed God to be fair and just, but also demanding, like any of the great princes she had met, but perhaps even more so.

More demanding. Yes. Much, much more demanding.

But she also knew, with a deep comfortable certainty, that God was a realist, that the world He had created was far from perfect – a fact of which He was keenly aware, and about which He himself was unembarrassed. And why should He not be? It was not an accident. Nor was it evidence of God's failure. He had made us imperfect. He had made us unequal. And she was sure He had done so quite intentionally – to give us all a challenge in life. To make us strive.

Of course He was fully aware that in doing so He had created flawed individuals. Even Mother Church had the occasional warlike pope and its fair share of lascivious cardinals, dishonest bishops and incompetent priests. So when it came to choosing a confessor – a role she saw as similar to choosing an advocate before you stood in front of a judge – it was important that you chose a good one, one who was intelligent enough to understand, knowledgeable enough to interpret correctly and sufficiently unbiased in his own daily life to present your case to God fairly and in a sensibly balanced way.

Under these circumstances, Girolamo Savonarola's sudden appearance seemed to be an opportunity that had not presented itself before. No priest in Florence could safely be trusted to take the true confession of a Medici. Not when the family had so many enemies, all scheming to replace them in the power structure of the city. But an outsider? A complete stranger? That was different. And not only an outsider, but clearly a zealot. Still with the full confidence of youth? It was surely the best opportunity she had found yet and she had been looking hard enough.

How serious were the sins she had to repent? Had she been so wrong to do the things she had done? To call it a "life of revenge" (a phrase she had heard in one of her nightmares) was, she thought, over-melodramatic, but she was aware there was more than an element of truth in that sentiment. In later years, certainly, a life of resentment. And therefore, if you understood her character, necessarily a life of active, almost productive, resentment. If you feel that strongly about something, it is wrong – almost immoral – to let matters lie.

Of course, if you measured everything by effects rather than by motivations, then even Piero – even, could you believe it, Contessina herself – might now thank her for what she had done. But her motives might sometimes, she had to acknowledge, have been somewhat suspect.

And Cosimo? Would he now thank her if he was still alive? Looking back, it seemed that in the end they had been on the same side, although it had not felt like it for much of the time.

So yes. She would do a deal with this young monk, and hope

22

that Benvisto did not return with anything too damning. There would always be risks. Always reasons not to act, reasons to wait, to continue looking for a better alternative. But life did not always offer better alternatives. Sometimes you just had to grasp the opportunity as it passed by and accept it. Especially when time was running out.

But she wouldn't make it easy for him. This Savonarola would have to work hard for his insights. Confession, as she had already told him, was not an act of charity. It always came with a price. Or at least, with a considerable expectation.

She decided not to beat about the bush. 'Yesterday, you offered me a trade: my unravelling of the intricacies of the city and commune of Florence in return for the salvation of my soul. It was an intriguing offer. But how will I know that you can deliver your side of the bargain?'

He shook his head. His expression was calm and confident, his eyes level and unwavering. 'You don't. But I do. And each day, as you impart your truths to me, you will prove it to yourself. For day-by-day, you will feel the burden of misrepresentation easing and your own soul will tell you that you are on the right path.' She went to reply, but before she could do so, he continued, and this time, he even had the temerity to point a finger at her. 'And you? How will I know that as you unpeel the onion that is Florence for me, the tears in my eyes are for the truth and not for the discomfort of having been misled?'

This time she could not resist pushing back at him. This competitiveness on both of their parts would, she knew, play an important part in their relationship. 'You will know. Your nose will recognize the truth when you smell it.' She took a chance, pointed a finger back at him, mimicking his own action. 'You weren't given that great nose without some purpose, were you?' And this time, to give him his due, he laughed. Encouraged, she pressed forward. No one knew the extent of her illness. No one, least of all this young monk, knew the urgency she felt. She must secure the best terms for the arrangement now. There would never be another opportunity like this one, and never a better time.

23

'I can offer you an arrangement. I will explain the truths and realities of Florentine life to you. But I shall do so in passing, by telling you of the events I have experienced in the form of a history, then where I can, how they were caused and how their final outcome came about.' Again, she pointed an accusing finger. 'But I will not do so in the form of an interrogation. Not even as a conversation. I withhold the right to tell the story my way and in my own manner. You will not interrupt me. Nor will you ask me supplementary questions, except on points of information. Instead, you will act in precisely the role you proposed to me, as my independent priest, taking my most private confession, according to the rules of the confessional.' The pointing finger became a fist. 'And under no circumstances will you write them down.'

Savonarola nodded once but she was not satisfied. She knew that such a simple nod could not be taken as final acceptance of her offer. It was clear from his expression he still had questions to resolve.

Here came the first. 'Where will these conversations take place?'

She smiled to herself. She had the upper hand now. He was accepting her conditions. 'There will be many confessions and all of them will take place during our month-long stay at Bagno à Morba. On each occasion I will send for you and you will come to me, in a private room, where we shall neither be overheard nor interrupted.'

He nodded. 'And afterwards?'

'After that, we shall not speak of these matters again. Before we begin, you will swear on the bones of Saint Dominic himself that you will not divulge the things I have told you to anyone. If you do, you accept that you will be burned alive and your body will be buried as an excommunicate.'

This time, Savonarola looked a little shaken. It was clear he had not expected quite such tough terms.

'You agree?' Lucrezia's eyes were level and she knew that they were telling him if he did not agree to these terms now, there would not be another chance for negotiation. He had two choices:

take it or leave it.

He read her expression and nodded again. 'Yes. I accept your terms.'

Lucrezia reached behind her. She had a travelling case, which contained her account books, her breviary and her bible. She took out the bible. It was leather-bound in the blue of Tornabuoni and had the Medici *palle* and shield embossed in red and gold leather upon it, a unification of the two families, as befitted a wedding present. 'Swear upon the book.'

Even now, he was careful. He opened the book in two, three places, ensuring from its contents that it was indeed a bible. He looked at her without expression and placed his hand upon it. Then he lifted his head and waited.

She dictated the phrases and he repeated them. 'I swear ... that everything I hear ... in our series of confessional meetings ... shall be held secret unto me ... shall not be written down ... shall not be divulged to any person ... living or as yet unborn ... and that if I break this oath ... I shall be burned alive ... and my body buried excommunicate.'

'Now kiss the book.' He did so.

Lucrezia returned the bible to its case. 'We leave in an hour. The next two days' riding through the *Colline Metallifere* will be steep and hard work. This morning we shall travel by way of Monteguidi to the Rocca di Sillano, near Montecastelli, where we shall rest. Tomorrow we shall pass by way of San Dalmazio to Montecerboli and thence to the Bagno à Morba. Once we get there, I will require about two days in which to complete my business and then I will be ready to talk.'

Savonarola bowed and turned to leave.

'Until the fifth day, then. And remember; none shall hear of this.'

By the time he reached the outer door, she was already immersed in her packing.

Chapter 3
Family Matters

He had been called. In an upstairs room of the guest house that Lucrezia reserved for herself and her family, Girolamo Savonarola took his place.

And waited.

To his satisfaction, the room was plain. The walls, though plastered, were un-frescoed, the floor of plain terracotta tiles and the ceiling of plainly-dressed chestnut beams and boards. Yet it had a comforting and welcoming atmosphere and as he looked around him, he realized that it was the warm golden light, streaming in through the large, south-facing window, which he had to thank.

Despite the welcoming atmosphere of the room, he found himself beginning to regret swearing to such stringent terms, beginning to question whether this woman really would tell him a concise and consistent story of recent events in Florence, and whether, in the process, she could help him to understand how that elusive society truly worked.

But what was the alternative? He had no one else he could approach. And besides, a deal had been struck, so now, surely, he must make the most of it.

Lucrezia entered and, without further ado, pointed him to a chair in the corner of the room. He sat. Immediately, he began to realize that the chair had been placed so that there could be no distractions. From where he found himself, Savonarola could not see anything out of the window. Instead his full attention would have to be on the woman in front of him, whether she sat in the chair she had her hand on now, or was pacing up and down the room as she had been doing for the past few minutes while he settled himself.

Now she in turn sat. He watched her closely as she prepared herself. His first impression, back there at the roadside, had been something of a disappointment. She was smaller than he had expected from her reputation: slight, yet not notably slender, being, as he now confirmed, somewhat heavy-limbed. A figure he had felt at the time that could almost be described as insignificant. Yet he remembered now what she may have lacked in stature she had immediately made up for in posture, for she had sat her horse, notably straight-backed rather than slouched, as so many noblewomen seemed to be when riding side-saddle.

Nobility, he had thought, dismissively, at the time. But that had been before she had spoken to him, before he had experienced those hawk-like eyes upon him and that mind concentrating on his every word, and choosing her response with a precision that had shaken him from any lazy assumptions and made him, in turn, concentrate to the full.

During her short interrogation of him at Casole d'Elsa he had hardly any opportunity to look closely at her. The candle-light in her Castello room had been poor and, in any event, he had been far too concerned with saying the right thing and convincing her to talk to him at all to worry about what she looked like.

Now, for the first time, as she settled herself and placed her notebook and reading glasses on her lap, he found he had the leisure and the light and allowed himself to examine her features properly.

Her face was by no means beautiful, indeed not even handsome, being narrow with a long chin and an even longer nose. A strange nose, he thought. Almost but not quite like a duck's beak, low-bridged and then curving outward with a strangely flattened and pointed end. Her mouth could best be described as tight, thin-lipped, the very expression of silence. The eyes? He examined them as she sat, heavily hooded above and somewhat puffy beneath; small eyes (and, he supposed, short-sighted), careful if not distrustful eyes and, as far as he could tell, eyes without hint of merriment. *There will be little laughter in this room.*

A pious face, perhaps? Hardly sad but certainly serious in its evident pre-occupation. A face for receiving rather than giving. A face in retreat from the world: watchful, careful, uncertain, almost hesitant and, if one were to guess, the face of someone who is, or who has been, disappointed with at least some aspects of life.

Yet when she began to speak, as he remembered so clearly from their earlier conversations, he knew she would come alive and that plain exterior would quickly be forgotten. For it was then that the strength – the inner strength of the woman – would emerge.

He sat back and smiled inwardly. *It is not what she looks like that matters but what she knows, and what she thinks and what she says.* He knew her voice, although soft and quiet, would be confident and her opinions, once expressed, would be clear and concise and decisive. An impressive woman then; once understood. *A woman*, he decided, as she took her hand from the arm of the chair and folded it over the other in her lap, *to be under-estimated at your peril.*

Today she seemed nervous, but perhaps only with that degree of tension that infects a preacher before he goes before his congregation, aware that he has one and only one opportunity to get it right, to find the words, and to deliver them in a manner that will influence the crowd. It was a tension he knew well and it played no little part in the reasons he was here today.

It appeared that she was as aware, then, of the importance of the opportunity, as he was, and, in her own way, was equally tense. *Perhaps, after all, our conversations will be as important to her as I hope they will be for me.*

Lucrezia cleared her throat. 'In trying to understand my family, the city and commune of Florence in which we live, and the actions we have or have not taken during our lives, I would like you to take some things into account.'

Almost startled that she had begun speaking, he remained passive, not even nodding. He had not yet worked out his part in these conversations. *Absorb. Bide your time. Observe and think. Think, and remember.*

'No man or woman has complete freedom. We are all constrained, by history, by circumstances, by the world around us and particularly by the presence of those who are closest to us.' As she spoke, Lucrezia seemed distracted by a thought. She put her glasses on the table beside her and rose from her chair. She walked to the window and looked out, perhaps surveying her work in bringing back to life the thriving resort now spread out below them. Then she nodded to herself, a decision made, possibly, and turned back to him.

'In this life, you have to play the cards you are dealt. In Florence, perhaps more than in any other part of Italy, family, and I mean that in the widest sense of *parentado*, is everything. One generation shapes the opportunity for the next and early in life you have to make an important decision: whether to live within the prison cell of your parents' attitudes and actions on your behalf, or to break out.'

Deep inside he felt his heart flutter. This was closer to home than he had expected. It was only by concentrating hard that he prevented his mind from drifting back to his own break with his parents and the agony it had caused all of them. But Madonna Lucrezia was moving across the room and the movement drew him back to the present.

She paused, her hand on the back of her chair, and then turned. Again she walked to the window. Savonarola shifted uncomfortably in his seat. This was going to take a long time. She began to speak again, turning as she did so, but this time remaining by the window. 'Not all parental attitudes are beneficial. Our world is changing so fast that the previous generation is often left floundering by the circumstances we now face.' The expression on her face hardened. 'And not all parental actions are unselfish.'

He nodded inwardly, remembering how his father had tried to re-establish his own reputation by pushing him into a position in the Este Court.

But she was speaking of something different. 'Fathers as well as husbands presume to make decisions on behalf of others, and too many women spend their lives playing a hand of cards dealt for them by a man. Please remember that when you judge us.'

She crossed the room, seeming suddenly to relax after establishing her ground rules, and sat in the chair. Savonarola noticed the wince in her expression as she sat and wondered whether the rheumatism she had referred to as they were talking earlier was causing her pain, or whether she had sustained some injury.

'The advice I am about to give you may be the most important advice anyone ever gives you, regarding your proposed stay in Florence.' She looked at him intensely and he nodded, swallowing hard, listening. Concentrating. 'Remember this. When dealing with the Medici, things are rarely as they seem. My advice to you, Girolamo, is always to judge us by our actions and not simply by our words.'

As she said it, her eyes rested upon his, and opened wider. Wider than she had allowed them to do in their previous meetings. For a moment, she held him in a still, cat-like stare, and for the first time, he saw – really saw – the person behind them. His heart lifted. *Yes, this is the woman. I have chosen the right one. She sees what others do not and as a result, she understands the depth of things that others merely ponder over.* Yet at the same time, trapped motionless in that intractable gaze, he felt a silent shiver of fear. *Be aware, there will be a price for such capability. This woman will be no passive commentator. She is a participant in the world I am asking her to tell me about and as such she will be assessing me, judging me, making decisions about what to tell me and what impressions to leave in my mind.*

So began Lucrezia's story, in her own words, with Savonarola on his guard, repeating her phrases in his head, filtering, editing, already prepared to apply her advice to everything she said herself.

Immediately he wondered why she had agreed to talk to him in this manner, how he could find the actions representing the truths behind her words, words that, if he took her literally, she had already admitted might sometimes be false, and would always need careful consideration.

Lucrezia leaned back in the chair. 'I shall start seventeen years ago.' She smiled and closed her eyes as she searched for the memories. 'I remember the back end of that winter well. It seemed endless, hanging on, cold and depressing, affecting everyone.

'In early February there had been talk of an earthquake, somewhere to the north of the city, although none of us in the family remembered hearing or feeling anything in Florence. The snow up in the Mugello had been so deep that year that the confirmation did not come to us for weeks. The church in Borgo San Lorenzo, they said, had been damaged and a few small old buildings had fallen to the ground. But Borgo was beyond our lands in the Mugello, further north, past Il Trebbio and beyond Cafaggiolo, and we thought little of it. Earthquakes are, after all, not uncommon in this part of the world, and the city had been unaffected.

'Like everyone else, we were pre-occupied with the cold. The snow had begun falling shortly after Christmas and from that time onward it never left us. Not until the end of April. And then it only went because the winds were so strong that they blew the snow away from us. That spring there was no thaw, no melting snow, no flooding in the fields. Just dry cold replacing the earlier snow, the ground still hard as iron, and the Arno frozen solid for weeks on end.'

~

CHURCH OF SAN LORENZO, FLORENCE
Sunday 19th February 1464

'The snivellers are living up to their reputation.' Contessina turns her head to the open nave of the church, where the *popolani* are crowding together. 'It's disgusting. The noise from their snotty noses and their coughing is so loud you can hardly hear the choir, never mind the preacher.'

Lucrezia nods her agreement. Not for the first time she wonders why the Medici work so hard to give the pretence of democracy to such people. What do the *popolani* know of the great affairs of state? But Florence has declared itself a republic centuries before, and the city still takes such pride in its quaint belief that the rights of every man are being upheld, that it would be beyond heresy to suggest an alternative.

'Maddalena believes it's their diet that makes them so unhealthy. She says if wages were higher they would be better

31

nourished.' Lucrezia sees the anger rising in Contessina's face and decides to tease her even more. 'And then the churches would be places of silent worship.'

'Pah!' Contessina almost spits on the church floor in her disgust. '*Maddalena thinks.* I don't give a fig for what that slave woman thinks, or says. Her opinions are of no value whatsoever. I don't know why you waste time talking to her.'

'Her father was a highly regarded physician. If he was here, I don't believe Cosimo or Piero would suffer so from the gout. Apparently he cured almost all of the nobles in Palermo in his time.'

A sniff from Contessina. 'Who says so? Maddalena? I don't believe she's a doctor's daughter. Never have. Black slave, that's what she is. Only good for cleaning, if you ask me.'

Lucrezia looks around to see if anyone is listening, but the *ting ting* of bells is competing with the row from the congregation and drowning out any murmurs of conversation. She's used to Contessina's bigoted comments, and considers they only diminish her in everyone else's eyes.

'Cosimo's own physician would vouch for what she says. He knew her father. He has a great deal of time for Maddalena's medical knowledge.'

'Which physician?' Contessina's chin is high in the air, a sure sign she won't change her opinion now.

'Doctor Ficino. He told me himself.'

'Diotifeci? You mean Marsilio's father? Are you absolutely sure?'

Lucrezia nods, if only to hide her grin. 'Knew him personally. In fact, I've known him confer with Maddalena to ask about some of her father's more successful remedies.'

'Speak of the Devil.' Lucrezia waves as Lorenzo, looking and acting much older than his fifteen years, eases his way comfortably through the congregation and up the steps to where the nobility have set themselves apart. Giovanni is with him, as is Carlo, and so is Marsilio Ficino, Lorenzo's closest friend. 'Shall I ask him?'

Contessina turns away, red-faced. 'Don't you dare.'

She is saved from further embarrassment as the service begins.

~

Lucrezia stopped and half-rose from her chair, as if changing her mind, and then sat back again, although now more upright. 'But before we can speak of politics, I must talk of the bank, for at that time the Medici Bank was the seat of the family's power and for much, if not most of the time, it was Cosimo's quiet background generosity that kept the city solvent.'

Savonarola nodded. *People like you to nod when they tell you things. It confirms that you are listening and gives them confidence without actually interrupting their train of thought.* He saw the tiny reaction on Lucrezia's face and satisfied himself that it worked for her too.

She continued, already appearing more relaxed. 'I am sure history will remember Cosimo and his father, Giovanni di Bicci, as the great men who built one of the finest banks the world has ever known, and that view is, I am sure, entirely justified. But it is also incomplete. For I am equally sure that history will judge my generation as having destroyed what they had built up and such a judgement would be mistaken.'

Savonarola allowed himself a raised eyebrow and she nodded as if in confirmation. 'Incomplete, then. The seeds of the decline in the Medici Bank had been sowed by Cosimo and, to a degree, even by his father, Giovanni di Bicci, himself, long before.'

~

CASA VECCHIA, FLORENCE
11th May 1437

'Come, children. It is time for a special lesson. Your father is going to talk to you.'

Lucrezia looks at her brother Giovanni Battista and nods sagely. In the Palazzo Medici the phrase 'your father' means Cosimo to them too, as well as to Giovanni and Carlo and to Piero, although, being quite a lot older, Piero rarely spends time with his younger brothers or their adopted cousins.

Carlo and Giovanni Battista drop their wooden swords and begin walking dutifully along the corridor.

Giovanni runs across to Lucrezia and takes her hand. 'Come on Krizia. Time for another boring lesson. I hope it's not ...' he makes a loud snoring noise, 'banking practice.'

Lucrezia laughs, as she does at almost everything Giovanni says, then she pulls a serious face. 'Actually, I think it's quite interesting.'

Giovanni lets go of her hand and starts mincing down the corridor. 'Oh doo you? Actually? Well I think it's boooring. Actually.'

Happily she grabs his hand and they run up the stair to the *studiolo* two at a time, shrieking.

'Today I want to talk about banking practice.' Cosimo is sitting on a small stool and the children are arrayed around him, on the floor.

Beside her Lucrezia hears a gentle snoring noise and has to pinch her nose to prevent herself from laughing. She can feel Giovanni vibrating with laughter beside her, but dare not join in, or even look at him. There seem to be special rules for Giovanni. He is able to get away with blue murder. But Cosimo is always strict with her.

She looks at Cosimo and nods. It's what you're supposed to do when people tell you things. It's good manners. Maddalena has told her it's all right to do it. It doesn't really signify that you agree with them, but if you really disagree you have to cross your fingers behind your back. Then it definitely doesn't count.

Maddalena knows these things. Maddalena's special. You can tell because Cosimo treats her differently from everyone else. That's because, secretly, Cosimo is in love with Maddalena. Girls can tell these things. Anyway, where else would Carlo have come from?

'Never hang around the Palazzo della Signoria, as if it is the place where you do business. Only go there when you are summoned and only accept the offices that are bestowed upon you.'

Cosimo is repeating the mantra. She's heard it before. Many times. But grown-ups repeat things to children because they think youngsters can't remember things. But it's not true.

Giovanni says it's because they've forgotten they've told you before. Giovanni knows everything. The problem is, you can't tell when he's joking.

'Never make a show before the people but, if this is unavoidable, let it be the least necessary.'

Cosimo is still droning on. She catches Giovanni's eye. He begins rolling his eyes and rocking his head from side-to-side. He's managed to creep behind Cosimo's shoulder, so his father can't see what he's doing.

'Keep out of the public gaze and never go against the will of the people.' Cosimo repeats the phrases often, always verbatim, and treats them with reverence – like quotations from the scriptures.

Giovanni leans towards her and whispers. 'The Word of God the Father.' He looks at her with a cynical half-smile on his face. The blasphemy, she is sure, is intentional and designed to challenge her. Lucrezia listens and absorbs. There must be some reason why Cosimo keeps on repeating these phrases.

The problem is, as Giovanni was the first to point out, Cosimo doesn't always obey these rules himself. In the main, he follows his father's guidance. He always rides a mule rather than a horse and is careful to present himself as a member of the *popolari* and not of the *nobili* when they are out in public. But Cosimo's father married his son to a Bardi – Contessina's from one of the oldest noble families in Florence – and Giovanni says Cosimo will marry him to Lucrezia when they grow up. And she's proud of her Tornabuoni name. And you could hardly argue that the Palazzo Medici shows people that you're a commoner, can you?

~

Lucrezia looked up at Savonarola and smiled. 'So what they said, and what they did, were poles apart, and even as a child, I recognized that.

'Likewise with the bank. Giovanni di Bicci had established his Principles of Good Management, and in the year following Cosimo's exile, while he was still feeling the pain of that experience, Cosimo applied the principles even further. The careful structure of a holding company, itself a partnership and

35

being in separate partnership with each of the branches, was made secure by establishing each of those branches as an *accomanda*, a special type of partnership with liability limited to the extent of the invested capital and no more.

'Inside that legal structure the management was equally secure. The manager of a branch would be chosen from the ranks and always based on many years of proven ability. He would move from being a salaried clerk to his first management responsibility, his reward for the first time including a bonus reflecting the profitability of the branch. And once he became general manager of the branch, he would be made a full partner, his reward a share of the profits and wholly dependent upon them.'

Lucrezia eased her back in the chair and winced. Across the room Savonarola saw her expression and again wondered what had caused it.

'Protection, stability and motivation. They were all there in those early days.' She shook her head. 'But by the time I speak of, it had become very different, and in my opinion the blame can be placed in the lap of one man and one man only. During its period of expansion and profitability, the Medici bank had been run by Cosimo as sole director, employing Giovanni Benci as his general manager. But in 1455 Benci died and Cosimo, sixty-six years old and increasingly infirm, began to make terrible mistakes.

'His first error was when winding up the holding company.' Again she sat forward, but this time it was to raise a hand in explanation. 'He had no choice. As a partnership, it had to be terminated as soon as one of the partners died. But he did not replace it with a new holding company. Instead he made the *Maggiore*, the senior, majority partners within the family, individual partners in each of the branches.' She lifted her head and looked hard at him. 'This made them individually liable for any losses those branches incurred.'

'You mean they were personally liable because they were directly involved?' Savonarola knew little of legal matters and less about banking.

Lucrezia nodded rapidly, as if the point was obvious. 'Yes

36

exactly.'

She paused, appearing to have lost her train of thought and Savonarola made a mental note not to interrupt again unless it was really necessary. It was better if she talked freely and openly.

'The following year, he made matters worse when his younger son, Giovanni, was put in charge.' Savonarola could see a softer expression cross her face and, seeing his response, she shook her head. 'Please don't misunderstand me. Giovanni was lovely, a charismatic, fun-loving man who could charm the birds from the trees. I will have much more to tell you about Giovanni. Supportive things. Favourable things. But the one thing he was not cut out to do in life was to run a bank.' For a moment she paused, the smile still on her face, but then saw him watching her intently and hurried on. 'Cosimo knew that and should never have appointed him, but we all loved him and since Piero, as the eldest son, was certain to be destined to follow his father's political ambition, Giovanni was given the bank.' Again she shook he head and in her expression Girolamo could see regret and, yes, compassion.

'From the beginning it was a disaster and within three years Cosimo was forced to bring in Francesco Sassett, to help Giovanni by running the day-to-day operations. But that relationship only lasted for five years, until Giovanni himself died.' As she said the words, she gave her head a sharp shake, as if forcing away an unpleasant thought.

This time Savonarola tried not to respond. She looked at him to see if he had noticed and, seeing no response, took a deep breath and continued. 'It was a chance for Cosimo to appoint more professional managers to work with Sassetti, but instead he did the worst thing possible, and put my husband, Piero, in charge. If Giovanni was unsuited, Piero was a disaster. But even that was not to last and six years later my husband, in turn, died and Sassetti was left to run the bank alone. He is still there today and the bank, under his management, continues to decline.'

Perhaps angered by her own story, Lucrezia got up from her chair and began pacing up and down. She walked toward the window, then turned and glared at Savonarola as if, somehow, it was his fault.

'I can tell you this. He would not still be there had the bank belonged to me.'

She shook her head and tried to calm herself. She walked to the window and looked out, her elbows resting on the windowsill. Then, with a resigned expression on her face, she turned and smiled. 'But it didn't. And it doesn't. And there's no more I can do about it.' Between each phrase, she paused, each a long, deliberate pause, and Savonarola felt as if she was hammering the words into his head, one-by-one, establishing a principle that she considered important.

One thing is certain. She's not afraid to hold opinions, nor to express them.

'And before you ask the question I can see on your face. No. I do not entirely blame Sassetti. He could not help being a courtesan and an inadequate. I blame the man who appointed him, Cosimo himself.'

This time, Savonarola could not hide a frown. 'Courtesan?' The word seemed to slip out of its own accord.

Lucrezia shook her head at the interruption to her train of thought. 'He told people what he thought they wanted to hear.'

She continued pacing up and down. Her face was quite animated, her voice high and, as she paced, she wagged the first finger of her left hand as if to concentrate and retain what she was saying. Finally, she lifted her head. 'After that, through a succession of bad decisions, the weaknesses at the centre began to be reflected as weakness in the branches.'

~

PALAZZO MEDICI
12th April 1465

'Piero! It won't do. It simply won't do.' Lucrezia shakes her head at her husband and wonders why he can't see the point. To her it's so obvious. With Cosimo recently dead, Vernacci just resigned and her brother running their most profitable branch in Rome, the bank is collapsing before their eyes. And Piero can't see it. 'You cannot go on like this. The bank will become a

38

laughing stock and so will you.'

'I thought I already was. At least in your eyes?' Piero looks downtrodden.

'Oh Piero. Come on! Don't go all maudlin on me. You know why the Milan branch was established, specifically to support the Sforza family at the Court of Milan. And you know as well as I do that one of the ground rules that Cosimo had been given by his father and which he preached to both of us as children, *ad nauseum*, was that the bank branches would always tie their business to trade and should never over-extend themselves by making large loans to kings, princes and *condottiere*. Cosimo knew the risks. The Bardi, Peruzzi and Acciaiuoli banks had all failed for just this reason. Yet here we are, lending money as if it has gone out of fashion, to the Court of Milan and establishing what is, to all intents and purposes, a single-customer branch.'

Piero lifts his head. Apparently he has not lost all self-respect. 'I know. But at the time, Cosimo had his reasons. Good reasons. You know as well as I do that he needed the support from Milan to secure his position with the *Signoria*, and Sforza needed our money to secure his own position as Duke of Milan. And with the government here in Florence having no money, the bank *had* to pay.'

She shakes her head because she knows he is right. 'Yes I understand. But there are ways of doing things. You can't throw away all good banking practice just because of political expediency...' She pauses, thinking. 'Not unless you want to lose the bank? Let it go? But if you do, who will pay for the costs of government? Although...' For a moment she considers, but rejects the thought, and returns to her original theme. 'In any event, now it's got worse. You know what's happened. Since Accerito Portinari came from Venice he's effectively become number two to his older brother in the Milan branch. Yet this too is explicitly contrary to the operating rules of the bank. You've seen the rules. There's nothing new about them. They were written thirty years ago.'

Piero shakes his head. 'I admit it's wrong, but it was a technicality. Father couldn't have predicted what was going to happen next.'

Lucrezia looks to the sky for inspiration. How can her husband be so obtuse? 'It was obvious what was going to happen next. Cosimo should have seen it coming a mile away. He knew that under the legal agreement, if Pigello died, the partnership had to continue until the end of the contract, with Pigello's heirs. That's what the agreement said. Cosimo knew that. He signed it. It's not as if he didn't know who Pigello's heirs were, is it? *His minor children and their guardian, Accerito.* Wonderful! So now we've finished up with a malformed branch, run by a weak and inadequate manager, and in personal partnership with the *Maggiore,* leaving them, as individuals, and that includes you, by the way, personally responsible for its losses. Piero, it could hardly be worse.'

Piero lets out a long sigh. Lucrezia can see he has no answer and she does not expect one. Not in the immediate future anyway, but he has to face up to the seriousness of the situation and start putting some corrective measures in place. Otherwise…

She can't let him off the hook. Not until he accepts the seriousness of the problems.

'Rome is just as bad. And yes, I'm talking about my own brother. For years that branch was managed, and managed well, by Roberto Martelli, but in his absence, and yes, I know he had obligations as Podestà of Prato, you gave responsibility to Leonardo d'Angelo Vernacci.'

Piero nods. 'He was a good man.'

'I know he was a good man. That's the point I'm trying to make. But then, at the following New Year, Roberto decided to make some changes, didn't he? Including a promotion of my brother to look after bills of exchange and correspondence.'

'That was six years ago.'

'I'm coming to that. We all know the work given to Giovanni Battista was considered managerial work and, as such, it amounted to a promotion for him. Now I know Vernacci never liked my brother, and you know he had his reasons. He had to complain about his work often enough over the years, didn't he? So understandably, he didn't take to changes being imposed from outside while he was nominally in charge, and responsible for the branch. Naturally and quite rightly, he complained to Giovanni in his capacity as director of the bank.'

'I know all this.' Piero looks irritable, perhaps because he knows what's coming.

But Lucrezia is galloping now and does not intend to stop. 'Yes, I know you know. War broke out, didn't it? And my brother decided he was being wronged and, without my knowledge, he complained about this apparent mistreatment to you. He wrote to you, didn't he?'

'And I replied, almost immediately. I took your side and your brother's. I wrote to Vernacci to argue Giovanni Battista's case.' Piero's voice is plaintive.

'I know you did. That's the point I am making. You should not have done so. It was completely inappropriate for you to do anything. Giovanni is running the bank, not you.'

'But I'm head of the family.'

Lucrezia shakes her head in despair. 'What's that got to do with it? The Medici Bank is a legal entity, with a partnership agreement, appointed directors and branch managers and a proper reporting structure in place. It's not part of the family.'

'But we own it.' Piero looks bewildered.

Lucrezia shakes her head in despair. 'Then you speak to the director of the bank and put your point of view, quite rightly, as one of the partners. But you don't stick your nose in and override the management.'

'But nothing happened.'

'No. Not then it didn't. But then, six years later, Roberto died and then so did Cosimo. In the spirit of the headless chicken, you still postponed a decision, which left the most profitable branch of the bank without leadership and with festering disagreements within.'

'Yes, that's true, but then in March, Giovanni Battista wrote to me and threatened to resign because he said life under Vernacci was impossible.'

'Yes, and what did you do? Against my strong advice, you played the dutiful husband, obeyed the obligations of *parentado* and put family before professionalism.My brother got the job and Vernacci, an excellent manager, was sacrificed.'

Piero shakes his head. 'Isn't that what I was supposed to do? I'm your husband and he's your brother.' He shrugs his shoulders. 'It all seems quite straightforward to me.'

Lucrezia opened her hands in supplication and frustration. 'Do you wonder that the bank is in decline now?' She stood at the window and pointed down to the efficiently-running business below, stabbing with her forefinger.

'Look at this. I know how to run a profitable business. And, as I am sure you know after talking to my staff, I know how to support a team of managers, how to give them authority, and how to motivate them to run the business profitably on my behalf. If you went to Pisa and spoke to Francesco the Goldsmith, who looks after my affairs there, you would get the same reply. So don't blame me for Cosimo's failures in later life.'

It was not a comfortable ending to their first conversation, but as Girolamo Savonarola walked back down the staircase, he was clear about one thing. He understood now how this lady thought and what made her passions boil. Yet something didn't ring true. Why did such an apparently confident lady feel the need to force her opinions upon him quite so assertively?

He was also left with a surprising and, to him, an uncomfortable possibility: that the bubble of reputation around Cosimo de Medici might one day be pricked and the reality found to be very different.

Chapter 4
Cosimo is Dying

He arrived at the agreed time, entered the room slowly and expectantly, and sat in the same chair. Then he waited.

The woman who joined him ten minutes later, disconcerted, her face drawn, her hands fluttering, was not the same woman who lectured him the previous day. She looked as if she had hardly slept, and kept pushing back her hair, hair that immediately returned to its position across her eyes.

She crossed the room towards him and put a hand on his shoulder. It was clearly an apology, although whether for her lateness or her unkempt state he could not tell. She gripped his shoulder once, and then went to her chair, turned and sat. She attempted a smile, but after the forcefulness of her manner the previous day he was not inclined to sympathy, and he remained impassive.

Rapidly, she began talking. 'Before we go any further, I think I need to redress the balance of our conversation yesterday.'

Savonarola sat, motionless and expressionless. *Take it slowly. Do not interrupt. I may learn something from her distress.*

Already, facing him, she was beginning to calm. 'I may have left you with the conclusion that Cosimo was not as great a man as he is remembered by most people.'

Still no response.

'I would not like you to cling to that thought. He *was* a great man and he *did* achieve great things in his time. The problem lay not with him, but with his sons: Piero, my husband, and Giovanni, my brother-in-law. It is true that in the period I was describing to you yesterday Cosimo was ill, frail and with far less capability than he had had in previous years. But he recognized that reality and he was more than ready to hand over his responsibilities to other people.'

Again, she tried to force a smile. 'His problem was that he could not find anyone suitable that he trusted to hand them to,

43

and in particular his sons let him down. I know this because he admitted it to me.'

Once again, the lock of hair fell across her face, but now, seemingly back in control, she pinned it back before continuing.

'It was in the July of 1464. There was plague in the city and I was taking the children to Cafaggiolo, and relative safety, when I received a message. Cosimo, it said, wanted me to attend him at his bedside at Careggi, as we were passing. I knew he was dying, they had told me so, and it seemed there were things to be addressed.

~

VILLA MEDICI, CAREGGI
July 1464

'Madonna Lucrezia, you are here.'

'Cosimo sent for me. They say he is dying.'

'In here.'

She enters the room. Cosimo is propped up, in bed. The room is dark and hot. It stinks, the stench of unwashed old men.

'Good God. What is this? The man will suffocate in this atmosphere. Open the curtains at once. And throw open the windows. He needs air.'

The servants shuffle ineffectively. 'The doctors will not let us open the curtains. They say the light will harm him.' Contessina is hovering; ineffectual as usual.

'Stuff and nonsense!' Lucrezia pushes the servants aside, throws open the curtains, and opens the windows wide. The expression of pleasure on Cosimo's face as the light and the fresh air reach him makes her whole journey worthwhile.

He clutches her hand. 'Lucrezia. Thank God it's you. Literally a breath of fresh air. You're the only man amongst them.' He beckons her close and, with a tortured smile, points to the Medici arms, with their six palle. 'The only one with real balls.' He waves a weary arm. 'Clear the room.'

Everyone except Contessina shuffles out, some more reluctantly than others. Cosimo signals with the backs of his fingers to his wife. 'You too, my dear. Don't take it personally, but I have business to discuss with the next generation here.'

With a disdainful sniff, Contessina leaves the room, but forgets to close the door. Cosimo points to it and with a grin, Lucrezia walks across the room and closes it firmly.

'I have an admission to make to you.' His voice is weary and downhearted.

'I have lost all faith in both of my sons. I was aware of Pietro's limitations from his very early years.' Lucrezia gives a little frown. The family had stopped calling him Pietro on his twelfth birthday. For a moment she wonders whether Cosimo is delirious and sees Piero once again as a lost little boy. She looks up and shakes her head.

'I did many things to try to build him up,' Cosimo says, 'and others to protect him from the harshest vagaries of this world, but nothing worked. He just did not have it in him. He was a terrible disappointment to me, and he still is, although nowadays I try to hide it.'

And then he says something she finds deeply upsetting. 'My greatest sadness is not the inadequacy of my eldest son but the fact that during his childhood I allowed my disappointment to show, to the point where Pietro was fully aware of its extent. That awareness of his failure in my eyes has, more than anything else in his life, been the thing that has held him back. It broke his young heart and now I know he will never regain the self-confidence he so strongly seeks. Even with your help as his wife, I know he will always remain a broken man and that I, in my desire to see him succeed and even surpass me, am as much as anything the reason for that destruction.'

She puts a hand on his, knowing how hard he will have found it to say the words. She tries to show her understanding with a smile.

'I know now that the exercise was futile' Cosimo says, his voice beginning to fail. 'The future lies with Lauro.'

This time she is less surprised, the whole family had called her son Lauro until he decided that he had come of age. That had been five-and-a-half years earlier, on his tenth birthday.

'I have made provision for him. When Lauro comes of age or,

if it comes earlier, when Piero dies, you are to take Lauro to the Convento di Santo Damiano. Maddalena is there and she will tell you everything. Maddalena knows everything. She will tell you what to do.'

The effort seems to have exhausted him and he lies back on the pillows. For a moment, she thinks he has gone, but a slight breeze makes the muslin inner-curtains lift lightly and she sees a small smile cross his face. Gently, she takes her leave.

~

'Those were almost his last words to me. To me they had a terrible finality.'

Lucrezia looked up and Savonarola saw tears welling up in her eyes.

But as he watched her, he could not decide whether her tears were of sympathy for her dead husband or sadness at the old man's revelation or simply tears of frustration that Cosimo had allowed such a situation to happen in the first place. She walked to the chair and sat facing him, a sad and distant smile on her face.

'Maddalena was Cosimo's slave for thirty-five years or more. I can't remember exactly now. She was as close to him as any person I ever met and in the end he had put his trust in her completely. He didn't know then that Maddalena had already died, and nor did I. Nor did any of us. It turned out that she had died in the February of that year, but nobody had told us. I only found out later. The memory of her seemed to drain him; as if he knew he had unfinished business and was ashamed of himself for not completing it.

'He said little more. He was too tired. But as I was leaving he called me back. "I am sorry that in my concern for the family, I came between you and Giovanni," he said. "It was one of the greatest mistakes of my life. All I can say in my own mitigation is that I had the interests of the family at heart. I was concerned that when I died, Piero would face great responsibilities as head of the family and, knowing his weaknesses, I believed that your strength was what he needed to support him. Now I know it was a mistake. Piero is inadequate and always will be. I should have allowed you to marry Giovanni. You would have been such a handsome couple, and made such beautiful children together."'

Lucrezia swallowed hard and nodded, emphatically. 'That's what he said. Then he closed his eyes and slept. The next time I saw him, he was in his coffin.'

Chapter 5
Cosimo's Funeral

'Yesterday I mentioned Maddalena. She had been Cosimo's slave and had borne him a son, Carlo, who now holds high rank in the church.'

Savonarola frowned. Carlo de Medici? He knew that name. A cardinal, a newish one. But he hadn't realized that he was the son of a slave. Then he remembered that the cardinal is black, yet with blue eyes. His mother must have had the same distinct colouring. Cosimo had brown eyes. How remarkable. What other secrets were going to emerge from these conversations? Now he was glad he had started returning to the privacy of his room each night and writing out copious notes on what he had heard that day. Lest his mind forget, of course. For personal use only, not to be shown or divulged. It did not break their agreement. Well, not the spirit of their agreement. Well, probably not. Did it?

She took a deep breath. 'It was at Cosimo's funeral, in the great church of San Lorenzo, that I first heard that Maddalena was dead. Her son, the cardinal, told me himself. It could not have been under worse circumstances.'

~

CHURCH OF SAN LORENZO
Thursday 2nd August 1464

'What did you say his final instructions were?'

Lucrezia is looking round the packed church. San Lorenzo is the *gonfalon* church of Leon D'Oro and the family church of the Medici. But it's not her family church. The Tornabuoni chapel is in Santa Maria Novella and, try as she may, she can't drag her allegiance away from it.

'Carefully understated.'

Piero's face is quite straight but she knows he sees the cynical side of it. Another example of *watch what I do, not what I say* … even if it is understated. And they could, she supposes, have paraded round the whole city, taking in all four quarters and every *gonfalon*, it is still, she is sure, quite different from what Cosimo had wanted and instructed. But then again, the survivors somehow always think they know better, don't they?

She nods and looks sideways at her husband. 'Carefully understated?'

'It was meant to be a small affair.' Piero is talking out of the side of his mouth. He's always been nervous in his piety and feels embarrassed talking in church. 'A private family affair. That's what I asked for.'

She chances a glance towards him and sees the strain in his face. He's insisted on doing the organization himself and she's aware it's tried his every capability. She's seen his accounts. Ninety-four pounds of candles for putting in the church. Another 96lb of wax for torches carried by the priests and a further 97lb to provide the sixteen torches surrounding the body.

And not just any old wax – it's best beeswax. Mind you, it does smell better. There's nothing worse than a church full of rancid wax smoke.

And then there are the candles for the thirty days of masses to be sung afterwards. How the chapter and priests of San Lorenzo will manage to use another 170lb of wax candles for those she can't understand. But no doubt they have to burden the rich to help lighten the load of the poor.

And then there's the mourning cloth. Four slaves and five maids at 6 yards each seemed reasonable, with the same for thirteen gentlemen and officials. Another eight women including herself and her daughters required 9 yards each, as did each of the twelve men from the family, including Cosimo's three sons. The only one who stood out was cousin Pier Francesco, who needed 11 yards, but he's been fat for years now and will go the way of Giovanni if he's not careful.

And then, of course, there's Contessina. She looks across at her mother-in-law. Yes we know she's in mourning, but 20 yards and 8 inches of black cloth and eight separate veils and two kerchiefs of black silk is, surely, overdoing it a bit? She looked like a trawler as she dragged that lot through the church.

Once this is all over Piero will start moaning about the expense. Still, he's probably managed to do a special deal on a candle wax order of that size and all that cloth will have come wholesale. Surely?

She risks another look round. All the family officers are present: the canon, their doctor, their chancellor and the factors and stewards from Careggi, Fiesole and Cafaggiolo. In all twenty-five men. All nine women seem to have turned up. She can see Contessina, Maria Nannina, both widows Ginevra (Giovanni's and cousin Lorenzo's), Laudomina, Pier Francesco's wife, and three others from the Vernio family. And for completeness, the five maids and all four of their remaining slaves, all, it must be said, looking very clean and smart.

What a pity Maddalena's not here. She would have enjoyed this, especially the gossip afterward. For one moment just now she had looked round, expecting to see her. With a stab of pain down her left side, she realizes how much she misses Maddalena. Such an enigma. A slave in law, but a friend in reality, to everyone except Contessina. She wonders how she fares in the convent.

She takes one more look round. Across the church, a nice touch she thinks, someone has invited a few of the artists whose work has so glorified Cosimo's life and who over recent years have been so close to them that they think of them as family. Michelozzo, of course, and Donatello are in the pew opposite hers and Sandro Botticelli, who has been living with them in the Palazzo Medici for the last two years, is beside them. Before the service he seemed quite overcome, but later, as they entered the church, she saw him laughing with Lauro, so he must have made quite a quick recovery. But then, when you are only nineteen, and sure you are invincible, funerals only seem to apply to other people.

~

Lucrezia had stopped speaking and was facing the window, but Savonarola could see her eyes were still far away, focused elsewhere.

'Quite a crowd in the end, but it was nice of them all to come.'

Suddenly she turned towards him. 'Of course, the one person who we all recognized was missing was Maddalena. We knew that once committed to a convent she could not easily gain a dispensation to leave, not even to attend Cosimo's funeral. But seeing Carlo in the cortege, I went up to him afterward and asked if he had heard from her recently.

'I have to admit I was embarrassed when he told me she had died six months earlier, when the earthquake, which, to be honest, we had not taken too seriously, had brought down part of the chapel roof in the Convento di Santo Damiano. The abbess, he said, had written to inform him of his mother's death, but he had assumed we would all know already, so had not written to us himself. "I thought my father always knew everything," was his comment, made somewhat acidly I thought. We all said a prayer for her. It seemed a bit late to do anything else.

'Cosimo's funeral itself was mercifully short, as was our walk home across the piazza. Later the *Signoria* decided that they wished to make some official recognition of his passing and passed a law declaring that in future he should always be referred to as Cosimo *Pater Patriae*.

'There was, of course, an element of fear and uncertainty throughout the city. Many saw it as the old order passing and they wondered what the future would bring. We could hardly tell them that we had the same worries and so had Cosimo before he died. Nevertheless, many, both within the family and outside, knew that Cosimo's death would leave a vacuum, and so, indeed, it turned out.'

Chapter 6
The Party of the Hill

'When you look back at it from the perspective of old age, life no longer seems like a steady continuum of day-following-day but more like a series of memorable phases, some long and some short, but each with a character and perhaps some lessons of its own. But the strange thing is, most of these phases, and certainly their significance, are only visible with hindsight. At the time, most of us had little sense of the new eras beginning, although as I look backward now, most of the endings did leave us with a recognizable sense of finality.

'I think that is why, with hindsight, we often appeared so unprepared, because at the time we were already deeply immersed in a new era before we had even sensed its existence. How advantaged must be the man who, early on, recognizes the opening of a new era and who has in his mind some measure of its likely direction and implications.'

Across the room Girolamo Savonarola nodded his head and willed himself to remember what Mona Lucrezia had just said. If only she would allow him to write it all down as she spoke. His memory, he knew, was prodigious by the standards of most men, and secretly he made his notes in the evening. But with someone like Lucrezia it was important to capture the specific words chosen and not just the general spirit of what she was telling him. Sometimes there was so much clarity in her head, and she did so often seem to be able to convert it into the right words.

Yet at the same time there was also something else, something that, although he only saw infrequent glimpses of it, appeared to contradict that clarity, as if she had some great uncertainty – some unresolved issue deep in her mind. The apparent self-confidence that he had seen at the beginning of their conversations was now starting to appear more fragile, as if she had, hidden away, some question of her own, a question that she was afraid to ask, perhaps because she was afraid of the answer.

In the quiet of the evening he had also found himself asking a recurring question. *Why did she agree to participate in this series of confessional meetings with me?* If that was, indeed, what they were in her mind. What had she said? What's in it for me? She must have asked herself that question. So what answer had she found?

He had replied and, he thought, confidently enough with his usual offering. But was that what had motivated her to continue? Something, he felt instinctively, was missing.

He was brought back from his questions by her voice. 'The period after Cosimo's death was a case in point. We knew what had ended, and when, and how, but we had little conception of what lay ahead, and even less how we should prepare for it.

'Piero was the least able to prepare for the future. He was the last of the old school – those who tried, at least in part, to follow the creed laid down by Cosimo's father, Giovanni di Bicci. But Lorenzo, or Lauro as we called him at that time, had made the break; at least in his head. Even at the age of ten Lauro knew that being a banker would stifle him. He was born to be a prince and that is what he was always going to become.'

There was something about the decisive set of her jaw and the *(had he imagined it?)* triumphant tone of her voice as she said the words that made Savonarola wonder how strongly the young Lorenzo had been influenced by his mother. And why.

~

'I would talk to you of January 1459.' Suddenly her voice seemed distant.

'In the spring of that year Pope Pius II visited the Palazzo Medici, and although Benozzo Gozzoli had yet to begin work on the *fresci* in the Chapel of the Magi, he started in the dry summer months and finished it that same year, the pope pronounced the building *a palace fit for a king*. I thought it was an interesting phrase, when used to describe a building created by someone with Cosimo's creed. But as I have said before, judge us by our actions, and not by our words. It was another, and final, example of Cosimo saying one thing and doing quite the opposite, and the pope had recognized it for what it was.

PALAZZO MEDICI
18th January 1459

'Lauro!'

Lucrezia stands at the foot of the stairs and calls her son. He appears and begins to descend. He is in his best clothes, including the scarlet silk *farsetto* and tight black hose his grandfather has just given him for his tenth birthday. He looks older – perhaps fourteen, and dresses, stands and walks like a grown nobleman. Half-grinning, he raises an eyebrow. 'You called, mother?'

'Galeazzo Maria is here.' She points to the open door through which the sound of arriving horses can clearly be heard.

'I know. I was watching from the window upstairs.' He reaches her and puts a friendly but firm hand on her arm. 'And it's Lorenzo from now on. Remember?'

She nods and goes to apologize, but he's already crossing the hall, hand outstretched, to welcome the Duke of Milan's fifteen-year-old son. They embrace laughing, and sweep back into the hall and up the stairs, immersed in conversation and without even acknowledging her presence as they pass.

Lucrezia smiles. Proud young nobles. They are already impressive. Soon they will be formidable. And then, in all probability, they will start to compete with one another. Galeazzo Maria is the sort of boy married women love: tall, slender, with shoulder-length curly red-gold hair, a strong aquiline nose and huge adorable eyes. Already he's beginning to build a reputation as a ladies man.

She checks with the housekeeper that appropriate refreshments are on their way then follows the boys upstairs to the new chapel. What a pity the fresci have not yet been started. Another couple of months Gozzoli says, once the walls have dried out from the winter weather. You can't fresco onto damp walls. The new plaster won't stick properly. She accepts that.

Four hours later, and the visitors are preparing to go. Lucrezia stands in the doorway and waves while Galeazzo Maria mounts his huge white charger. She has to admit he's every inch a *condottiere's* son and will look like a duke even before he becomes one. Beside her, Bianca, Maria and Nannina are all pulling faces at each other. It seems the duke's son has made a good impression.

The visitors leave and Lorenzo, thoughtful, calls to a servant. 'Where's Apollonio Baldovini?' He turns towards her, shaking his head. 'Did you see that horse?'

~

'Within a week Lorenzo had sent his head groom to buy a stallion just like it. He said to me, "Mother, the future is clear. I am going to be a great prince. Greater even that Galeazzo Maria and my horses will beat his at the *palio*. You watch me." And everything he said that day became a reality, so some of us, at least, could see forward into the future.'

'And Giovanni? Your husband's younger brother?' For the first time, Savonarola took a chance and asked a question. He waited, hoping that Lucrezia would not end their conversation. But it was a genuine question. More than once she had hinted that Lorenzo took after his uncle rather than his father. If there had been a fundamental break in the family's purpose, from bankers to princes, where had that break occurred?

Lucrezia hesitated. It seemed the question had been unexpected and had stopped her flow of thought. But although she seemed to understand the reason for asking it, her delay in replying suggested she was undecided how much she could tell him.

And as a result, he listened twice as carefully.

'You are right to interrupt, and I forgive you for it. Your question is a good one. As I was saying before, we are often clearer about the end of one era than the beginning of the next. My husband, as we both know, represented the last dying embers of Giovanni di Bicci's influence. Lorenzo was of the new school, the school of princes, and yes, it was from Giovanni that he inherited that new attitude.'

'Giovanni was a strong influence then?'

She smiled, nodding. 'A very strong influence. He and I had

been brought up the same way. We believed in the same things. Change was in the air. Unlike my husband, neither of us had a strong reverence for the past. We were far too busy trying to build a future.' She looked at him carefully, clearly choosing her words. 'Besides, when your father is not only cold but remote, and distant, and inattentive, your uncle, if he is close, may become the main male influence on your life.' She grinned. 'Especially when he represents fun, and opportunity, and enthusiasm for life. And Giovanni was all those things.'

'You and he were childhood friends, were you not? Close friends?' He sat back in his chair, trying to look relaxed, hoping, despite her ground rules, that she would ease her rules and allow further questions.

Lucrezia smiled, a weary smile of resignation, as if someone had tried to creep up on her by tip-toeing past an open window. It was almost a smirk. She shook her head in amusement. 'Our rule is becoming damaged isn't it? I thought I said no questions?'

He heard the words, but he also read the smile and he took a chance. 'On a point of information only, *Madonna*. Hardly a question. But clarifications? They, surely, may be permitted?'

Still smiling, she tipped her head from side-to-side, as if considering his proposal. 'For a monk you are a good swordsman.' Lucrezia's mouth was open and she had her tongue in one cheek, perhaps to suppress an open laugh. Her eyes were merry and bright and it was clear she was enjoying their duel of words. Finally she nodded, a decision made. 'Agreed, then. Points of information and clarification are permitted.' She raised an admonishing finger. 'But you are not to lead the conversation by active questioning.'

She tilted her head to one side, as if to emphasize that the diversion was at an end and that she was intent on returning to her original theme. 'As I said, we were brought up the same way and we believed in the same things. Shared beliefs can create strong bonds.'

Savonarola watched her carefully. There was tenderness in her eyes. What was it that made her face soften in that manner? He would have liked to ask more, but he knew he was at risk of spoiling a developing trust and that at this early stage, he should not push her further. If there was something hidden in her mind that she felt the need to confess, he was sure it would emerge. Eventually. Given time.

Patience – that's what was needed now.

Lucrezia paused, clearing her throat, trying to regain her direction. 'And that brings me back to where I started, with the great hollow after Cosimo died.'

Across the room, he was sure he could sense relief, now that she had pulled the conversation back to her original theme. So what had been the diversion that, finally, she had managed to avoid? He would think about it when he made his notes that evening,

'The problem was, while we were looking at ourselves and trying to decide who and what we were, others were laying more active plans and seeking change. Piero thought he had inherited a calm situation, one which Cosimo had had under control. But the loss of Giovanni, who was universally popular, followed by the death of Cosimo, who was at least universally respected, had started to trigger uncertainty and after that, almost everything Piero did seemed to increase that uncertainty, rather than damp it down.'

Her eyes drifted across the room 'Mind you, being carried around the city in a litter because his gout was so bad was hardly likely to drum up confidence, or additional support, was it? And when word leaked out that the London and Bruges branches of the Medici Bank were both on the edge of bankruptcy, well, as you might expect, matters got distinctly worse.'

On the other side of the room Savonarola nodded his understanding, as he was sure she expected him to. But the thought in his mind was not of appreciation for her clear analysis, but rather surprise at the extent to which she despised her late husband. But it was a sensitive subject and he made an effort not to let it show on his face as he lifted his head again to listen.

She continued, appearing not to have noticed. 'They called the Medici *reggimento* "The Party of the Plain", because we were based in the *gonfalon* of Leon d'Oro, along the Via Larga. Now it became clear that we were weakened and all eyes began to shift to the other *reggimento*, the so-called "Party of the Hill".'

She tipped her head on one side in explanation. 'The hill refers, of course, to the Monte alle Croce, although Pitti's *palazzo*, where they were based, was right at the bottom of it, in Oltrarno – in fact, almost on the edge of the old Bardi streets.

'The actions Cosimo had put in place meant that the Medici could not be voted out of power and we had for years relied on Francesco Sforza and his armies in Milan to protect us from a violent attack.' She lifted her eyes again 'You will remember I told you about the Milan branch being established for the sole purpose of lending money to the Sforza Court? Well now you can see what was happening, how the financial interests of the bank were becoming compromized by the need to maintain political stability in the city.'

Again he nodded, although he was not sure he shared her interpretation entirely. 'Are you telling me that Cosimo was using the bank's money and risking the bank's future, to buy peace in the city and, would it be true to say, to provide his own protection?'

Her thin smile failed to hide the glare in her eyes and he knew his arrow had found its target. But she seemed unwilling to concede the point further and instead continued bravely on. 'In any event, eighteen months after Cosimo's death, Sforza died and we suddenly found ourselves vulnerable.

'Unusually for him, Piero reacted quickly this time, and sent Lorenzo to Naples to argue our case for protection with King Ferrante. To our delight he came back smiling, saying everything had gone well and that King Ferrante had pledged support. But Naples was a long way away.

'Then, in August, Piero was struck down by a particularly bad case of gout, and taking what turned out to be poor advice from his friend Diotisalvi Neroni, he decided to retire to Careggi.

'It was then that they struck.'

~

CAREGGI
August 1466

'Father! A messenger. He looks concerned. Better come quickly.' Lorenzo, as always, is the first to notice the new arrival.

The messenger looks exhausted,his horse lathered and his clothing covered in dust. 'I have come from Giovanni Bentivoglio, Lord of Bologna. I am to tell you that you are about to be attacked. Two armies are on their way, one from Venice and the other from Ferrara.'

'How close are they?' Lorenzo has taken charge, as usual.

The man gulps his reply. 'Close, my lord. Eight hundred men under the banner of Borso D'Este, Marquis of Ferrara, have already been seen, passing through Fiumalbo.'

'Headed this way?'

'Yes. They say they have instructions to capture Piero and to kill him.'

'Diotisalvi Neroni. The bastard. He's misled me. He advised me to come here. He must have known this was going to happen.' It's Piero, dressing as he attempts to run.

'We must return to Florence. They've played the same trick they played on Cosimo, thirty years ago.'

By this time the whole household is up and dressed. Lucrezia calls for food for a journey. 'Quickly.' Lorenzo sees to the horses. Piero limps inside and gathers up his papers.

Within the hour, pausing only to scribble a note to Galeazzo Maria Sforza, who has become Duke of Milan on his father's death, and another to the citizens of Arezzo, asking them also for their support, they set off by the direct road.

Lorenzo, now seventeen and brimming with self-confidence after his recent success negotiating in Naples, decides to ride ahead. He comes toward the village of Sant' Ambrogio del Vescovo. As the name suggests, the village belongs to the Bishop of Florence. At this time the *vescovo* of Florence is Giovanni Neroni, Diotisalvi's brother. So as Lorenzo approaches the village he is particularly on his guard.

He turns to one of his small band of companions. 'The village is too quiet. I smell a trap. Hold back behind this wall and observe. If you don't get the all-clear from us within five minutes, ride back and tell my father to go round the other way.'

Sure enough, as they enter the narrow streets they are pounced upon by armed guards bearing crossbows. Lorenzo and his men un-sheath their swords and begin to fight them off. And as they do so, their lone companion quietly turns his horse and rides back to warn Piero to take another route.

When he needs to, Lorenzo can talk his way out of a locked chest. More than that, he can do so in Latin, in the silky Italian of diplomats, or in the rough Tuscan of the streets. It's the street Tuscan he uses now. He recognizes the men. In the past he and Carlo have often played street football against them. And being Lorenzo, he is confident he knows how to handle them.

'What the hell are you doing, lads? Put those fucking bows away. You'll hit my horse. And it's worth a dozen of you useless fuckers.'

'Where's your father?'

'The old man? Oh he's miles behind. Pissing about trying to fix the wheel on a cart. Silly old sod. If you want to talk to him, he'll be along in about an hour. Loads of time. You've got time for a second breakfast. In fact, if there's any girls around, you've got time for a quick screw. Talking of which, I'm on a promise myself, back in the city. Got to go. See you!'

In the confusion they let him go and he rides with all haste to the Porta Faenza and into the city. Once there, and confident that his father has been warned, he finds himself amongst Medici supporters and begins to rally them.

Savonarola realized he was sitting on the edge of his chair. But Lucrezia, who was walking up and down and waving her hands, was in full flow and he had no intention of interrupting her.

'As soon as Piero arrived, matters began to turn. We did not know it at the time, but it appears that at the moment they heard that Piero had avoided capture, Agnolo Acciaiuoli, Niccolò Soderini and Diotisalvi Neroni rode off from the Palazzo Pitti with the excuse of gathering up their men. Apparently, they were in such a hurry that they left Luca Pitti alone – an old man, wondering quite what had happened.

'It is clear now that his nerve broke, because a short time later, he arrived at the Palazzo Medici, hot and terrified, pleading for an urgent audience with Piero, who had barricaded himself in, surrounded by armed men.'

~

PALAZZO MEDICI
August 1466

They bring Luca Pitti to Piero as soon as he arrives. Three of the soldiers throw him to the floor and stand over him with open swords. He looks terrified. At seventy-four years of age, he is unused to such treatment.

As soon as they meet, he crawls pathetically to his knees and swears that he has been misunderstood. 'I've always done my best to prevent violence,' he pleads. 'Piero, you must believe me, I've come here to warn you of the situation.'

Lorenzo has his blood up and no time for weakness. 'He's lying. He's in the thick of it. Chuck him in the street and let the masses cut his throat.'

But Piero, bless his heart, has known Luca Pitti all his life. He likes the old man. Always has. So he forgives him, and pardons him for his sins.

Luca, exhausted, sits there weeping, as Lorenzo, disgusted, puts on his armour and heads for the stables and his charger.

~

Savonarola watched her expression as she turned and walked back toward him. Once again he could see she did not agree with her husband's decision. Somehow he could never see her and Lorenzo giving Pitti such an easy escape. But no doubt they had had their reasons, probably to do with *parentado* once again.

Almost immediately, she confirmed what he had been thinking. 'Just to be sure he didn't change his mind again, Francesco Sassetti, our general manager at the bank, pledged that Luca would marry his daughter Francesca to someone close to Piero.' She snorted. 'Of course, Luca thought he was referring to

Lorenzo himself.' Then she began to smile, shaking her head gently. 'He was pretty upset when, a year later, we married his daughter to my brother Giovanni Battista and packed her off to Rome.'

She paused in her pacing, and lifted her eyes once again. 'Always read the small print. That's what it's there for. Even in an oral contract.' And just in case he had missed the joke, she winked.

Again, he nodded, ostensibly in acknowledgement. But he knew it was another lesson to be learned and remembered. *These Medici must be like live eels to deal with.*

'From Pitti we learned that his co-conspirator, Niccolò Soderini, had sent word to the Ferrarese army to ride straight into the city. He told us Soderini was planning to go to the Palazzo Vecchio to bully the *Signoria* into arresting Piero. So just to be safe, we sent word to Galeazzo Maria Sforza to ride towards us as quickly as possible, and broke out the arms from the armoury under the roof in the Palazzo Medici to protect ourselves.'

Finally, Lucrezia slowed her frenetic pacing, and returned to her chair. She sat down and helped herself to a glass of water. Then, looking tired, she smiled.

'But nobody came from the *Signoria*. We learned later that, in the confusion, nobody had actually been given the responsibility to do so. Either that or whoever had been told to do it decided to forget his instructions and to lose himself in the streets.

'Then word spread from reliable sources that the army from Ferrara had turned back, and that the Venetian army, it seemed, had never even left home. Now, by this time, we had three thousand troops of our own surrounding the Piazza della Signoria and matters started to swing back our way.

'The following morning, we rang the *Vacca*, the great cowbell in the tower of the Palazzo Vecchio, and summoned all mature men into the Piazza. Then, with Lorenzo riding up and down in full armour and our troops with drawn swords, we sorted out the true men from the others and let them into the square. The rest we sent home.

'The *parlamento* began in what we insisted was the proper legal manner, and we asked for a *balia*. Needless to say, with only our own men in the square, the shout of approval went up immediately and the *balia* was formed. It wasn't hard. We already had a hundred names ready and confirmed in advance. The emergency committee sat and immediately agreed the death penalty for Acciaiuoli, Neroni and Soderini. As is the custom, the aggrieved person was then allowed to speak and Piero, showing both humility and mercy, requested that their sentences be commuted to ten years in exile, which was universally approved.

'And in that manner, peace, once again, was restored.'

Lucrezia paused, easing her back, and took another drink of water. 'Democracy in Florence has its own ways of working, but we manage it, somehow.'

She smiled and the young monk bowed his head low. This was not a time to make comments or to ask questions. He had learned a great deal and now his priority was to get to his room and to start writing his notes, before he forgot everything.

Chapter 7
Lorenzo's Choice

As he climbed the stairs to their meeting room the following morning, Girolamo Savonarola found himself pausing, looking out of each window as he passed it, and thinking.

He was conscious of preparing himself, somehow sensing that the ground rules had changed and that, from that moment onward, their conversation had the capacity to lift itself onto a higher plane – onto a new level of mutual respect and understanding – and in so doing might begin to open the doors to those secret places that so far, he believed, had remained hidden and withheld from him.

The previous afternoon, some hours after their daily conversation had come to an end, he had found himself sitting on a high wall, overlooking one of the larger pools, watching Lucrezia and her guests taking the second of their three daily treatments.

The process had seemed comfortable enough, almost, to his eye, self-indulgent. But then everyone's life seemed self-indulgent to him. Most days they would assemble by one of the pools. Then, dressed lightly but still modestly in long cotton robes, they would immerse themselves in the warm sulphurous water of the pool. That apparently being the sum total of their physical activity, they would then set themselves the task of relieving the boredom of the next two hours, and for this either music or conversation seemed to be the starting point.

But the previous afternoon, the conversation had flowed almost entirely in one direction, as Lucrezia had been talked into reading from her long poem *The Life of Saint John the Baptist*. Of course she was not the first person to have taken the single verse in St Mark's Gospel and turned it into an extended story, either in the form of rhyming *stanze* or of the religious plays, most commonly put on in the streets on feast days and called *sacra rappresentazione*. But she was, almost certainly, the first *woman* to have done so.

She had read about fifteen *stanze* when he realized that he knew the poem verbatim. Thinking forward he had suddenly recognized that an opportunity was about to come to him. Carefully and unobtrusively, but moving as fast as he could, he climbed down from the wall and made his way round to the side of the pool. They had not seemed to mind his presence and he had taken a seat in the shade of the same wall, leaned back, and listened, waiting for his moment.

She had been one third of the way though the poem when he prepared himself for his opportunity:

> *O son what words are those that you say?*
> *Why do you wish to abandon us so quickly?*
> *Will this celebration endure for such little time;*
> *This feasting we make for your return?*
> *The request you make of us is hard, O son;*
> *Why do you wish to leave us?*
> *O son do not put us through these trials;*
> *Please stay with us and may God bless you*

Surrounded by high walls on three sides, the pool acted like an amphitheatre and Lucrezia's voice was loud and clear. As she reached the last line, he knew his moment had come and, speaking from memory, he stood and walked forward, toward the edge of the pool:

> *I have told you and I tell you again*
> *Why I was sent into the world;*
> *So that I may go, a mendicant, into the desert,*
> *And live cheerfully in a state of penance.*
> *Let me tell you yet again;*
> *I must go alone into the most obscure*
> *Place that there is. Please rejoice with me*
> *That I go to fulfil God's commands.*

As he reached the end of the *stanza* he hesitated. Perhaps they would think him presumptuous to have interrupted in so direct a manner and especially in presuming to speak the words of The Baptist himself, and in front of the author.

But Lucrezia's smile had told him all was well. She had recognized immediately why he had chosen that part of the poem to interject. And although not every citizen of Florence might accept the description of their city as a desert, she knew it described fully the position in which he thought he found himself.

Little more had been said. She had introduced him to two of the ladies he had not met before and he had been invited to remain, sitting beside the pool, and to share the rest of their entertainment. But he knew that to Lucrezia a greater communication had taken place, that she had recognized he knew her poem off by heart and that it had offered him the opportunity to declare his innermost vision of his own place in the world. And in being able to do so through the words of her poem, he had found a deeper affinity between them than either had previously recognized.

Now, climbing the stairs, he felt a sense of trepidation. If the previous day's events had opened the door to an inner sanctum, would that door remain open or would she, with a night to think about it, have decided to close it once again? She was, he was sure, a private person at heart.

He knew the start to that morning's conversation was important. And for that reason, he must be careful not to appear too eager, too presumptuous.

Her expression as he walked in gave him some relief. 'Good morning, Girolamo. How well you quote my humble poetry. Your point of entry yesterday was, if I may say so, inspired.'

He grinned, nodding. 'Thank you. I was grateful for the opportunity, *Mona* Lucrezia. Given the circumstances it was something of a gift. Even as you were speaking, I remembered the first time I read that *stanza*. It was in Ferrara and I had just been transferred to the Convent of Santa Maria degli Angeli as Teaching Master of Novices. I thought then it described the way I thought about my situation better than anything else I had ever read, and I still think so to this day.'

Lucrezia looked at him, he thought gratefully. He had written enough to know that there is no greater reward for a writer than to be told your writing has captured the essence of a moment for somebody else.

'Do you really see yourself out in the wilderness?'

For a moment he wondered whether, once again, he was being teased, but the question appeared more kindly than probing.

He paused. It was an important question, especially when asked by someone as perceptive as *Mona* Lucrezia. 'As an Observant Dominican you will know I have already put myself outside the world of possessions. In that respect, I have made myself an exile to the society in which you live, with its *palazzi*, its golden churches, its sculptures and its fine paintings. But in the last two years it seems my own interpretation of the Observant Order has also placed me outside the fold of much of Mother Church, which, as you know well, continues to embrace such possessions itself.'

Lucrezia nodded, her expression seemingly understanding. 'You have strong principles, but I fear your rigid adherence will make your life difficult, especially in as unforgiving a city as Florence. Already I can hear you being ridiculed by the masses.'

He frowned, the insult seeming unnecessary, and with her face softening, she explained. 'Please hear my words carefully. My comments reflect the prejudices of the city, not your competence, which I am unable to judge. But you are, if I may point it out to you, a Lombard, with the high nasal tones of Ferrara and, as such, I promise you, you will be treated by the people as a foreigner.'

She saw his expression intensify and shook her head. 'Understand me. I do not criticize. I merely state the facts as I see them and as, eventually, I know you shall experience them. Such distrust may be a measure of the people's own insularity, but you have to face the fact that when in Florence, you will be measured by a Florentine measuring stick.'

'By a Florentine ruler?' He grinned as he said it. The pun was far too good an opportunity to miss.

'By him too, *and* by his mother, perhaps.' Her smile remained kindly, but now not without a combative edge, and her forehead had gathered itself into a half-frown. 'We are all judged, daily. But some are more able to act on the basis of their judgements than others.'

Girolamo looked into those hooded eyes and could not decide whether she was threatening him. 'Your son is a very powerful man.' *When confronted by a more powerful dog, lie on your back and show submission.*

'My son is a prince. Both by choice and by necessity. And it is I who have made him so.' She pointed Savonarola to his customary chair and he sat. It seemed the theme for the day's homily had been selected.

'We spoke yesterday of the Pitti conspiracy. That was a turning point – for me, for the family and for the city. It was that event, more than anything else, which made it clear to me that there was no going back. Cosimo was dead and so was poor Giovanni. Now all that was left was the gout-ridden Piero and the already-magnificent Lorenzo, the end of the old and the beginning of the new. It was one occasion when I did know that we were on the cusp, not only of a new generation, but of a new era.' She was looking at him hard again. 'No doubt, like others, you will judge me harshly if I tell you that in my eyes history had already made its decision, that men already saw Lorenzo as the future and that a growing number of them already believed that Piero was finished. He was part of history and in the eyes of the people, and the only useful thing he could do was to die and take his rightful place in life's story.'

The eyes were more hooded than usual and fiercely combative. 'Does that shock you? To have a woman talk thus about her husband?'

He absorbed what she had said and considered it. With a deep sadness inside himself he remembered the two letters he had written to his father from Bologna, explaining why he had to leave Ferrara and break away from the path the family had planned for him. Those letters had represented the culmination of a similar battle – one between himself and his father.

~

BOLOGNA
25th April 1475

The desk is small, as is the student hovel it sits in. But he doesn't care. Not for him possessions, comforts, never mind luxuries. He has measured the world and judged it. Not long ago he decided to step out – onto the new path he has chosen for himself. Yesterday, during his parent's pre-occupation with the St George's Day celebrations, he did it. He left home and fled the city. Now, exhausted, he is here, in Bologna. Now the rest is up to him. He will either succeed or fail. But the success and the failure will be his and his alone.

All that remains is to cut the one remaining knot that ties him to the past – to his family. His beloved mother will know what has happened. Only two days before, as he sat, crying and lamenting the world to the accompaniment of his lute, she had found him and cried out, 'Oh my son, this is a token of separation.' He had not denied it. He had been unable to face her.

Matters cannot be left like that. However much he knows he must face the world alone, he cannot leave his mother grieving in uncertainty. Somehow, he must try to explain. He must write and tell them what he has done and why. But even as he embarks on the most difficult letter of his life, he knows they will never understand.

Nevertheless ...

Honoured father,
I have no doubt that my departure is very painful to you, particularly because I stole away so secretly, but by this letter I want you to understand my soul and will, so that you may take comfort from it and realize that I have not made this move in so childish a way as some people think.

His father had wanted him to seek a secretarial post within the Este court, but he had seen enough of that court through his grandfather, who had been court physician, to reject it, its wealth, its domination and misuse of others, its greed and its insincerity.

For a while he had studied medicine, influenced by his much-regarded grandfather, but in the end, after graduating in the arts and humanities at the University of Ferrara, he had decided where his moral compass pointed and he had left for Bologna and the church.

That rejection, of everything his father held dear, had been painful, but since that time, he had never once regretted his decision to face cold reality and to accept its consequences. But still he needed to try to explain his actions. He owed them that at least.

He looked up. 'Do your words shock me? No. Not at all. You spoke the truth as you saw it. I too have had to face harsh realities and their ineluctable implications. And, like you, I still feel the pain of so doing. But it cannot be avoided. Breaking out of an established convention is difficult, especially when it has been established by your own family. But what must be done must be done. There is no other way.'

Across the room he saw relief on Lucrezia's face as she replied. 'Then we understand each other and I need spend no more time in justification.'

She paused, seemingly gathering her thoughts.

'Lorenzo had returned from Naples full of confidence and when Pitti and the Party of the Hill rose against us it was Lorenzo who warned his father and he, also, who rode the streets on his great white horse in full armour, rousing the troops and almost single-handedly cowing the people. Once we had the city under control again and the plotters had been dealt with, I sat with Lorenzo, reviewing the past and looking hard at the future.'

Savonarola could tell from Lucrezia's expression that whilst she had been content to acknowledge her husband's limitations, she was uncomfortable talking openly about her son. Yet now she was making herself do it, and in so doing was opening a window on exactly the sort of detail he had hoped and prayed for.

She paused before continuing. 'I explained that he had three choices.'

PALAZZO MEDICI
6th September 1466

She stands with her hands on her hips and knows that this time she has her son's full attention.

'It's time to choose, Lorenzo. You have three alternatives. First, you can choose to concentrate on the money, to reorganize the bank and start running it properly, staying clear of city politics and concentrating on being a successful man of business.'

As she finishes the sentence, Lucrezia is already shrugging her shoulder, as if the suggestion is ludicrous. She knows that Lorenzo has given it short shrift in the past, and so is she, now. 'Do you really want to be a prudent banker? Of course not.' She flicks her eyes across the room.

Lorenzo almost sneers his reply. 'You don't even need to ask the question, Mother. I have been educated as a prince and that is what I intend to be.'

Lucrezia can hardly argue. She knows it has been his ambition since he was ten years old and he hasn't changed. But already he is seeing his ambition in a different light. He no longer wants to be like Sforza, Galeazzo Maria's reputation has been destroyed by the terrible tales emanating from the Milan court. Now Lorenzo is setting his sights higher. 'I shall be a greater prince than Galeazzo Maria ever will,' he had said to her recently, and she knows with certainty that he means it, and with equal certainty that he will succeed.

But for the sake of history, for the sake of their relationship in the future, and as her lawyers would say, for the avoidance of doubt, she recognizes that she has to present him formally with the alternatives and to hear him choose between them.

'The second choice is to do as your grandfather has done in the past, and as your father is still trying, but with increasingly disastrous results, to do now. And that is – to run the bank and to use its profits to support an active role in Florentine politics, whilst at the same time continuing to maintain the pretence of a true democracy.'

She shakes her head as she looks up. 'It is, as you may already

71

have gathered, a tightrope, stretched between expectation and resentment, both on the part of the people. On the one hand they expect the wealthiest citizens to dig deep in their pockets and to provide the joys and benefits of Plato's Republic out of their own money. But on the other hand, as soon as they are seen to do so, such men are attacked in the belief that they are seeking self-advancement and power over the rest.'

To Lucrezia's delight, Lorenzo's eyes narrow. She knows he loves this kind of debate and always learns from it. 'What's wrong with that? Cosimo managed to do it.' Yes, she has his attention now. He's thinking, and probing, and will remember the outcome of the conversation. All the more reason, therefore, to convince him.

The motherly smile appears. Lucrezia of all people knows that if you offer Lorenzo the choice between two things he always wants them both. So carefully, and not for the first time, she warns him about the difficulties of clinging to power in what the city of Florence cynically describes as its democracy.

'Cosimo managed to do it by his bleeding fingertips, although it cost him a fortune and he was exiled for his trouble along the way.'

'How large a fortune?' Lorenzo is motionless and looking at her like a hawk, really listening now.

She pauses. She should have known that Lorenzo would not let a loose remark like that pass unmeasured. Not when money is concerned. That is why she used it. And this time she is prepared. She has the answer to hand. 'Over his adult lifetime; six hundred thousand florins, all given to the city and to its churches, convents, and monasteries. It is the price we pay for our social position.'

Lorenzo whistles and his eyes grow wide, although he is careful not to say anything because he knows she has another point to make, and he is not going to miss a word.

'Your father is still trying to do it now,' she says, 'and is permanently on the brink of failure. It's an impossible task, and a thankless one.'

Lorenzo looks at her with one of his looks and she knows he

isn't entirely convinced. Not yet, at least. 'Why can't it be made to work?'

'Because the system is flawed. It is inherently weak. When the elders designed the system, they had two things in mind, and both were principles rather than practicalities. The first was a somewhat naïve desire to emulate the benefits of the old Greek democracy – giving power to the people, not recognizing for one moment that most of the people have no idea what to do with power if they have it, or how to exercise it effectively.'

Lorenzo understands that, and he grins. 'Or responsibly. And the second?'

'Their second objective was to establish a system that prevented any one individual from becoming Prince of Florence. So they arranged for new elections every two months, not recognizing that it takes longer than that to get to understand the issues to be addressed and the means at the government's disposal.

'Furthermore, being mean-spirited in their endeavours, and again wishing to prevent any one person from becoming all-powerful, they failed to provide adequate funds for the government process. As a result, two things have happened.'

Lorenzo tips his head to one side, listening, and raises one finger.

She nods. 'Yes. First, there is, even to this day, no permanent bureaucracy, not even an adequate team of book-keepers and clerks, so nothing can be done with any efficiency.'

Lorenzo nods his acceptance and raises a second finger.

'Second, because of the lack of resources, then and now, the only men who can achieve anything are those who have resources of their own – and thus we come full circle. The leaders, and by that I mean our family, still have to pay for the process of government themselves.'

Lorenzo is motionless, looking at her, thinking, absorbing.

She goes for the kill. 'That situation cannot continue. The world is changing and changing rapidly, and Florence needs to change with it. To hold power and to drive through the processes of change that will be necessary, you will need to be a strong prince.

Lorenzo looks hard at her. 'Do you *really* mean that? What you just said? You know it is completely against grandfather's policy and my father's best attempts.'

She returns the look. 'I am fully aware of that. But the world is changing. Now it's time to face the new reality, Lorenzo. You will be a prince. A prince of Florence. The city needs it. And the republic needs it. Fear not. You can do it. You were born to be a great prince.'

Now, finally, Lorenzo grins and preens himself. And then he says 'Yes I was, wasn't I?'

For a moment, he pauses, and she wonders if she has convinced him after all. 'And the bank? What happens to that in your scheme of things?' He opens his hands. 'I assume we are now pursuing your third option?'

Lucrezia raises an eyebrow, almost in surprise. 'The bank? Why, it is time the city learned to pay its own way.' She jerks her head to one side, as you would tell a horse to walk on. 'Be a prince. Lead them to the greater glory they so desperately desire, but this time, you must make sure they pay for it themselves.'

'And the bank? Grandfather's beloved Medici Bank?'

'Oh make no mistake, Lorenzo. The bank is in terminal decline. But if the profit of the bank only has to finance the Medici family and not the whole Republic of Florence, then it will probably suffice.'

She sniffs, dismissively, in the manner she so often uses to end an argument, and turns away from him. 'Let Sassetti and the others run it. They can't do any more harm than they've done already and as a great prince, leading a mighty city and state, which is paying for itself, you won't need it any more. Turn your back on it. Let the bank go hang.'

Across the room, Lucrezia stopped pacing up and down the room and for the first time that day, sat down, opposite her confessor. She opened her hands and smiled. 'And that's exactly what he has done.'

It was later that day, in the quiet of a receding afternoon, and Girolamo Savonarola had been walking, high in the hills behind

74

the cliffs of the Bagno, upstream, where the gorge narrows and the eagles fly undisturbed. As he approached the bunkhouse where he had chosen his simple accommodation, he met Piero Malagonelle, looking pensive.

'Ah!' He paused, waiting.

'Mona Lucrezia was looking for you. She's in the hotel, talking to the manager. She asked me to tell you, if I saw you.'

He nodded his thanks and continued down the path. She was where he was told she would be, studying the account books with careful concentration.

'Ah! It's you. I hoped to catch you before we met tomorrow. I should like to change the rules, the basis on which we meet and have our little talks.'

He smiled and tipped his head to one side, to signal receptivity without making any specific commitment either way. 'As you wish. What is your proposal?'

'I have two. First I am willing to relax the *no questions* rule. You have satisfied me that we think along similar lines and now we have made some progress together, I should be willing – indeed I might go so far as to say I would encourage – some questions from you.'

'Thank you. I shall do my best not to abuse the privilege. And second?'

'I notice you have been walking. Like you, I like to walk, and after a week here in one place I feel in need of a change of scenery. Perhaps tomorrow, instead of sitting face-to-face, we might take a walk together?'

He waited for the catch. There must be a price for this generosity – surely? But no conditions were forthcoming and after an awkward pause, he nodded his agreement. 'It's a good suggestion. We shall walk tomorrow, and I will try to think of some questions. Until then.'

Even as she walked away he expected her to turn and present him with a condition, but none came and he continued down the hill, wondering.

Chapter 8
Patrons of the Arts

'This was a good suggestion.' Savonarola paused, allowing her to catch up. They had been walking for nearly half-an-hour, in the main without speaking, but aware of each other's company and enjoying the sun, the morning breeze and the scent of rosemary and jasmine all around them. In the many years she had been coming to the Bagno, Lucrezia had never climbed this high above the valley before. Now she was finding the fresh air and the exercise exhilarating.

'I agree. Fresh air is always beneficial. And talking as we walk should be ...' As the word came into her head she paused, uncertain that this was, after all, the direction she wanted their conversation to take. She knew they were not intended that way, but with an earnest young monk like this one there was a risk he would find her comments heretical.

'Should be?'

He's a sharp one this. He seems to recognize that I am trying to escape something and the very recognition seems to make him want to pursue the matter more diligently. She decided to take the risk. 'Less confrontational. Talking as we walk should be less confrontational.'

'But until today, we have spoken as if we were in the confessional.' His expression looked bewildered, but the focus in his eyes told her the bewilderment was pretence, and a ploy. 'Do you really find the confessional confrontational?'

She paused. *This is risky. With such a zealot I could be on dangerous ground. But why should I retreat?* She decided to press forward and in so doing to explore the depth of his piety. 'Oh worse than that. On occasions I find it positively inquisitional.'

She saw the word strike home, as it had been intended to.

But he remained firmly in control. He stood and looked at her carefully. 'Really? Then tell me. Is it the *persistence* or the *intensity* of the questions that confronts you?'

She smiled, once again hearing an echo of her own training in rhetoric, now long ago and, she had thought, long forgotten. Interesting that he should have avoided the word *inquisitional* and returned instead to *confrontation*. A nice attempt at entrapment too, to presume that the source of her feeling of confrontation must either be persistence or intensity. But to her it was an old lawyer's trick and easily avoided. She could lead him a merry dance with this if that's what he wanted.

She tipped her head to one side, giving his question the consideration that it deserved. 'Either, I believe, could create an uncomfortable sense of invasion, but I think it's more a question of enclosure.' *There. Let's see what he makes of that.*

He dropped the pretence of bewilderment. Now he appeared fascinated, his face animated, his smile combative, almost flirtatious as he responded. 'How interesting. But enclosure can, surely, bring a sense of inclusion, of sharing?'

She shook her head. 'Not face-to-face, through a grille. That, in my mind, suggests conflict.'

'And the converse? What is that and how is it to be nurtured?'

She smiled, knowing she had won this little psychological battle, but at the same time relieved that they had turned the corner, that he had shied away from the risk of an argument with her and instead was now trying to see her side. To her it was an important step forward, one that vindicated her earlier decision to change their relationship from face-to-face across a silent room and instead to use the excuse of walking, as it were, to stand beside him and to ensure that they faced the same way. 'It can be nurtured by co-operation, by partnership.'

'By facing in the same direction?'

'Exactly so.' *Thank goodness. The exact phrase.* She hoped her relief was not too obvious.

There had been more than one occasion during their recent meetings when she had felt a growing chasm between them. Brief moments but nevertheless worrying. If this young man was to act as her confessor, then it was essential that he understood her and the nature of the world she had lived her life within. If he was to stand in judgement over her, the simplistic mind of a

77

radical needed to be tempered by a clear perception of Florentine reality. Now, at last, it seemed, he was willing to listen.

They reached a level area on the path where a break in the undergrowth offered a long view across the valley. A view, it seemed, appreciated by someone before them who had conveniently built a bench to sit on. They took the opportunity to sit – as they said, facing in the same direction, in partnership.

Lucrezia pushed her wind-blown hair back from her face. 'Do you like the countryside?' She waved her hand, indicating the scene before them.

He looked, sniffed the clean air, closed his eyes, and then inhaled again, this time more deeply. A smile broke across his face and for the first time, beneath the unattractive exterior, she saw the face of an intense, intelligent and sensitive young man. He nodded, eyes still closed. 'As an alternative to cities, yes, always. John the Baptist went out into the wilderness and I think I understand why.'

She looked at him and frowned. *Is he retreating again*? But she said nothing. Perhaps she was being over-sensitive. *Give it time. Don't crowd him.*

He shook his head, answering her unasked question. 'To get away from people. To be clean.'

She frowned again, surprised and not a little confused. 'You find cities dirty?'

He nodded, then quickly opened his eyes, his face suddenly with an expression of great distaste. 'I have seen the city. It is full of vile bodies and filth, and corruption.'

His words were so aggressive she crossed herself. 'Oh dear. What makes you say that? You speak of Florence in this manner?'

'Specifically of Ferrara. Of the Este Court. My grandfather, Michele, was the court physician there. He told me of things. Disgraceful things. Disgusting things. The place is a whorehouse. A den of iniquity. A sordid pit of filth. A mire of moral degradation.' He turned to face her and, being so close, leaned back to allow his eyes to focus on her face. 'But I have no reason to believe that Florence is any better. Bologna wasn't.'

She looked at the anguish in his face and wished she could

help him overcome it. An intelligent young man should not be smothered by such negative thoughts. 'Do you think it possible that your grandfather exaggerated the situation?'

His face creased with anger. 'Exaggerated? No. He died when I was fifteen. But to the day he died, he always told me the truth. And I can assure you he did not exaggerate it. I have seen it for myself. It was worse than he ever described. Much worse.'

~

ESTE COURT
Late January, 1460

'Is that the pope?'

The eight-year-old holds his grandfather's hand and stares as the pope alights from his barge on the River Po and glides towards Duke Borso. Behind him, maintaining a respectful distance, are a handful of cardinals and a dozen bishops followed by an assortment of hangers-on and servants.

The party looks like an exhausted expedition, returning from a long and arduous journey, dishevelled, tired and downhearted. But as Pope Pius II approaches the duke, he manages to smile regally and offers the papal hand without trembling.

Two rows back in the small crowd, Michele Savonarola smiles down at his grandson Girolamo. 'Indeed it is.'

'How did he become pope? Did God appoint him?' The boy never stops thinking; never stops questioning.

'He would say so. But the truth is that when Pope Calixtus III died the cardinals were disagreed about his successor. The front runner, and by far the favourite, was Guillaume d'Estouteville, a wealthy cardinal from Rouen in France. But some of the cardinals hated him and so they sought an alternative. And the cardinal they disliked least was Enea Silvio Piccolomini.'

'Why did they choose him?'

Michele shrugs and sticks out his lower lip. 'He was, at least, Italian. From Siena. So apart from the Florentines, most people could tolerate him. He has some good points. A good orator, especially in Latin, and a much-travelled and experienced diplomat. But although he took the name Pius, he has little reputation for piety. He was, really, the least-worst choice in many of the cardinals' eyes.'

The boy frowns and his grandfather ruffles his hair. 'That's often how it happens and why the decision frequently takes so long.'

Girolamo nods and continues watching. 'He looks thinner.' The boy is always direct in his comments, but he is right. The pope has lost weight.

'He's had a difficult year.'

The pope's eight-month-long negotiations at the Council of Mantua, upriver from Ferrara, have drained him to the core. And by the end, he has still made no progress in convincing the Italian states that they should unite against their common enemy. Constantinople, it seems, will remain in Turkish hands.

'Why did they all go to Mantua?'

'The pope invited them to meet together. To make an agreement to fight the Turks, in a new crusade.'

'And did they agree?'

'No.'

'Then why is Duke Borso making such a fuss?'

'It's expected.'

Girolamo sniffs. 'There are less people with him than there were last year.'

'You're right. Last year there were ten cardinals and sixty bishops. And there were lots of princes as well as servants and dignitaries. Most of them seem to have gone now.'

'Why were so many there in the first place?'

'It's all show. To show that the pope is important. To maintain awe at his elevated position.'

'But why does Borso respond in the same way? Why is he too dressed in cloth of gold? Why are there rose petals spread about everywhere?' He shakes his head. 'The poor are starving and yet there is so much waste. It's disgraceful. Why does the duke allow it?'

'For the same reason. The Marquisate of Ferrara has never been of particular economic importance. And so, progressively, the marquises and now the duke have made themselves important by becoming power-brokers, negotiating settlements between the more important states. That way they sit at the same table and enhance their position. And, in passing, their wealth. But to continue to be seen as players in the great game, they have to show that they're important. And they do that by *magnificentia* – by show of wealth.' He winks at the boy and leans down to whisper to him. 'Even if they've had to borrow the money to buy all this finery.'

'So are they not really wealthy? Not truly important?'

Michele signals the boy to speak more quietly. Then he bends down and whispers again. 'Most of them are frauds. Not really of noble blood at all. Won their titles in battle, or stole them, or bought them.' He leans close to his grandson and puts his mouth to his ear. 'Last year, when the pope was greeted by ten great nobles all ten of them were illegitimate, including Duke Borso.'

'Borso's illegitimate?' Now even Girolamo is whispering.

'Yes. And he's not really a duke either.'

'No?'

'No. Not really. Eight years ago, the Emperor Frederick III made Borso a duke, but the title has to be renewed every year, and it's conditional.'

'Upon what?'

'Upon paying four thousand florins.'

'Can the emperor do that?'

'He can and he does. They all do. Last year the pope signed eighty appointments in one day: dukes, bishops, doctors, all sorts. And they were all paid for. That's how it works.'

'But that makes a joke of the whole thing.' Girolamo is looking up at his grandfather now. Michele shrugs. 'And why all the boys in white? And why are the river banks adorned with pagan statues? For a pope? It's blasphemous. Surely?'

'The statues represent pagan divinities.'

'Why?'

'To show they all pay homage to the pope.'

'But they aren't, are they? And they haven't?'

'No. But the duke pretends they have. It flatters the pope.'

Girolamo takes his hand from his grandfather's and puts both hands to his face. He rubs his face hard, as if to shake off a bad dream. Then looks at his grandfather again. 'So an illegitimate, rented duke pays dishonest third party homage to a pope nobody really wanted, and the pope pretends to be flattered and pleased. And they both do this, although neither believes in it, in order to impress the masses, who have paid for the whole spectacle with their taxes?' He frowns. 'Doesn't that mean the whole spectacle and the structure of supposed superiority it represents, are both deeply flawed?'

Michele Savonarola smiles and nods to his grandson. 'Yes. Exactly.'

~

Lucrezia frowned. During these moments when he fell completely silent, the boy's expression suggested real and terrible pain. She had painful memories of her own, more than enough of them, but to see such utter anguish.

'And your father? Did he, too, direct you away from the Este Court, as your grandfather had done?'

Savonarola shook his head, as if her question was ludicrous. 'You have no conception of what it was like there. Do you? It was impossible. Borso was succeeded by Duke Ercole. After that, the court of Duke Ercole dominated everything and everyone. Even more than Borso's had done before him. There was no question of fighting it. Not if you wanted to remain in Ferrara and make a living.

'Besides, my father was a nothing. A failure! There would never have been a question of his pushing me towards some other future. He didn't have the knowledge or the imagination. He just wanted me to take up a position in the court. It was the only way, he said. "They will welcome you there," he said.'

Savonarola shook his head in disgrace and resignation. 'Welcome me! What a joke.

~

SAVONAROLA FAMILY HOUSE, FERRARA
June 1471

'Girolamo! What is wrong? For two weeks now you have been

neglecting your books. It's not like you. Are you ill?'

He smiles to himself. Close as he is to his mother, this is one agony he cannot share with her. It's exactly two weeks since Roberto Strozzi and his family arrived in exile from Florence and moved into the big house next door. Exactly two weeks since the perfect Laodamia first appeared in their garden seeking to make new friends in a strange city.

Since that day he has done nothing but think of her. Every day he has contrived to meet her, to talk, even to walk home from church together. Today he will tell her. Today, knowing with confidence that he will have his parents' approval, simply on the basis of what he has heard them say about the illustrious Strozzi family next door, he will approach her and ask her, subject of course to the usual formal processes between fathers, to marry him.

Feeling sick with anxiety, he leaves the house, walks next door and knocks. He asks for her and, being recognized, is welcomed into the house. Now he waits, as she is called.

She enters the room, an enquiring look on her face. Has she guessed the purpose of his visit?

'Signorina Strozzi.' He bows, formally, as she surely expects.

She stifles a giggle. 'Please Girolamo, call me Laodamia. We are neighbours and friends, are we not?'

Encouraged, he bows again. 'Laodamia, since your arrival in Ferrara, we have spoken daily. And during that time, we have, I believe, developed a friendship.'

She tips her head to one side and smiles, says nothing, but the pink in her cheeks is encouraging.

'My family, as you know, is well-established in this city and, I would like to think, highly regarded. My education has been amongst the best and I have studied diligently. As a result, my prospects at court are, I am confident, excellent.' He sees a slight hesitation in her face but puts it down to shyness. 'You must know that during these weeks, I have come to hold you in the highest possible regard.' She reddens, but he continues. No time for hesitation now. The words start to pour out in a torrent. 'That being the case, I am here to ask you, and subject of course to the usual formalities, if you would do me the inestimable honour, of agreeing to be my wife.'

She puts a hand to her face. 'I? To be your wife? You must surely be jesting with me?'

He shakes his head. 'Not at all. It's just that …'

'I, a Strozzi, from the noblest family in the whole of Florence, should marry a Lombard? Someone from Ferrara? Indeed not a someone from Ferrara, but a nobody from Ferrara. Worse than that even, should marry a Savonarola from Ferrara? And as I can see clearly with my own eyes, a stuttering, impoverished, futureless, ugly, foul-breathed Savonarola at that? I think, sir, your joke is in bad taste. You must be out of your head, even to consider such a suggestion.'

'But I thought…'

'You thought wrong, sir!'

She opens the door and calls out. 'Maria! The visitor is leaving. Kindly show him out.'

~

To Lucrezia's amazement, and considerable discomfort, he put his hand to his mouth and bit the knuckle until it bled. 'She rejected me, didn't she? Laughed in my face.'

'She? Who laughed in your face?' Lucrezia could feel the pain in his voice and see it on his face.

'The Strozzi girl. *La Bellissima* they called her.'

'A beauty from the Strozzi family rejected you?'

'She was the most beautiful girl in the city, and a Strozzi, so under normal circumstances well out of my reach. But I had learned from my grandfather that she was illegitimate. Our family had fallen on hard times since my grandfather's day. My father had failed at one venture after another, and I knew our name did not stand for much. But if she was illegitimate … So I made her a proposal of marriage.' There was blood on his lip as he spoke.

'And she rejected you?'

'She laughed in my face. It was only months later that I discovered she hadn't been told she was illegitimate. But by then it was too late. The word was out. Everyone knew what had happened. Already I had become a laughing stock at court.'

'You were known at court?'

He paused, and then, as he went to speak, the corners of his mouth curled up and she saw venom in his expression. 'Oh yes. I knew the court and, as the bible says, the court knew me.'

Lucrezia shook her head. 'I don't understand.'

~

STREETS OF FERRARA
10th August 1471

It is a difficult and dangerous time. Duke Borso has died. He was without issue and in recent weeks the succession has become a contest between Niccolò, son of Lionello, and Ercole, the legitimate son of Niccolò III. There has been a fierce contest, culminating, eventually with open fighting in the streets. But last night, Ercole won.

Now is the time for retribution, for old scores to be settled. And now is not the time to be walking the streets of Ferrara wearing Niccolò's colours. As all of the Savonarola family still are.

'Well, if it isn't Girolamo!' There are five of them, grinning, but heavily armed and threatening nevertheless. 'Still wearing the old colours I see? No time to change, perhaps?'

Girolamo Savonarola shakes his head. Nobles. So-called honourable gentlemen of the court. Former friends of his father. He hates people like this. People whose allegiances can be bought and sold. He looks round but there's nowhere to run to. The only chance is to brazen it out. Today that doesn't look easy.

'Remind me. In the great contest between Niccolò and Ercole, which one won?'

Savonarola looks at the sneers and hopes that the right answer will save him. 'Duke Ercole.'

'Indeed he did. But not, as you may have noticed, without a fight. Look around you. The streets are running with blood.' One of them lifts a dagger to his throat. 'Including our blood. Dying of wounds inflicted by your friends, they are. Bad business.' Nods all round. 'We don't take it kindly when our friends are butchered.' Heads now shaking in unison.

'Makes you want to take revenge on someone.' A different voice, but the same tone and message.

Now the leader comes forward, balancing the flat of his dagger blade on his finger. 'Nice balance, this knife. Like the scales of justice. Balanced, see?' He holds up his finger so that the knife rocks before Girolamo's eyes. He feels his stomach turn over. 'You'll be pleased to hear we believe in justice.' The knife blade remains close to his face. Nods all round. 'A court of law. That's what we need.' More nods. 'A trial.'

They take him into a house and lock the door. 'This is a fair trial. Or at least as fair as our friends and colleagues got at the hands of your side in this matter.'

'But I haven't done anything. Nor have I said anything on this matter to anyone.' It is the first time Girolamo has spoken more than two words.

'Passive resistance, eh? That's even worse in my book. Those who just stand by and let it happen.'

A new voice. 'Allegiance. That's enough. You don't have to have done anything. Moral support is crime enough.'

'What crime do you accuse me of?'

'Treason.' The face is very close. The grinning teeth are filthy. The breath smells of stale wine.

'You are accused of treason, because your family has supported the side of Niccolò. Do you deny the charge?'

'I deny treason. I am a loyal subject.'

'Loyal to Niccolò. Yes. To the wrong side, to the losing side. That's the problem. And evidence enough, in our book.' The speaker looks round the room. Nods of agreement from the other four.'Well, that was easy. A unanimous verdict. This court finds you guilty of treason.'

A new voice. 'The punishment for treason is death by burning. However, we are short of firewood at the moment, so we offer to commute your sentence. We'll give you a choice.'

'What is the choice?' He can hardly speak.

A third voice now. It's as if they have been rehearsing. 'Death in contumacy or absolute submission. Take your choice.'

'Submit to what?' Perhaps they will respect him more if he stands up to them.

'To the will of the court.'

He knows them. He has known them all his life. Some are friends of his father. Some of their sons are his own friends. This cannot be real. Surely it's just a game. To make the point that their man has won. He hopes so.

'I submit to the will of the court.'

Smiles all round. Perhaps he was right after all? He prays he is.

'We must keep this legal. Sign here.' As he signs the document, without even reading it, they begin to smile again. He doesn't like those smiles. He doesn't like those smiles at all.

~

Savonarola's eyes were full of tears. 'I knew these men. They were nobles. They were friends of my father. They gave generously to the church. They were patrons of the arts and provided the city and its churches with paintings and sculptures. They were pillars of society. Yet they made me sign a legal document to the effect that I submitted to whatever they did in that room, and agreed to it by my own choice.'

He smashed his hand down on a rock, once, twice, three times, until she saw the blood flowing all down his arm and ran to stop him.

'And then they fucked me. They stripped me naked, bent me over a table, and one after the other, they fucked me. All five of them.'

And as Lucrezia watched, the self-confident young monk dissolved into a distraught and tearful boy. Instinctively she put an arm round his shoulder and pulled him to her. He gripped her *mantello* and pulled it to his face, as if to hide his shame, and silently she hugged him as he cried openly, while the blood from his smashed and bitten hand soaked through her over-cloak and into her *gamurra* beneath.

Finally, as if drained of all emotion, he raised his head to her, sniffed and wiped away the tears. 'But what you can never understand is that with all the pain and the degradation, I think I enjoyed it.'

It was nearly an hour before they resumed their walk and their conversation. An hour in which she tousled his hair like one of her sons, in which he apologized for the bloodstains on her clothing, and in which, with a look of abject pleading on his face, he asked her to promise never to divulge his secret to anyone.

She squeezed his shoulder in reassurance. 'It is my solemn promise. We are both bound by the rules of the confessional. Even out here, whilst walking. Now we are united by our secrets.'

Together, drained of emotion, they stood, and helped each other to continue their walk, for neither of them, she sensed, felt ready to turn back and to return to the people and the chatter in the valley below them.

'You have a long life ahead of you,' Lucrezia told him, as they resumed walking, albeit now much more slowly but still arm-in-arm. 'I would hate to think that your terrible experiences in Ferrara have soured your joy in all things creative, all beauty, just because they were enabled to come into existence by the power of the wealthy. Rich does not have to be bad and expensive does not have to mean ugly or debased.'

He looked at her, and she could see he did not believe her.

'Think of the pleasure you have had from reading. You told me you have read Cicero, Quintilian and Ovid.'

He nodded, as if wanting to please her, but seemingly unwilling to allow his pain to dissipate so easily. 'Latin as it should be written. But my preference is for the saints: Jerome and Augustine and above all, St Thomas Aquinas. In his writing I find truth and the greatest solace.' He lifted his head, an element of defiance returning. 'But none of those wrote for money. No rich benefactor caused them to write as they did. They simply sought truth.'

She nodded back, needing at this difficult time to agree with him. 'I too. But I also receive succour by looking at the architecture of Michelozzo Michelozzi, at the paintings of Fra Filippo Lippi, at the *fresci* of Giotto and the sculptures of Donatello. You cannot, surely, reject Brunelleschi's dome on the *Duomo* purely on the grounds that the rich merchants of the city participated in its funding alongside the poor?'

'You are trying to trick me.' His face was petulant now.

But she shook her head. 'Not at all. But you will need to be able to respond to such debate if you are to preach in the city of Florence. You may be right in everything you say, but the people of Florence are merchants, street people, market people, arguers, debaters, writers and negotiators of contracts, manipulators of the spoken and the written word. You will be in their city. Words are their pleasure and their sport and if you want to convince them, you will have to play the game their way.'

His eyes were like those of a chastised dog and she smiled as she used to do to her children. 'All I ask is that you do not sweep us all into the gutter just because we sponsor great works of art.'

He nodded, wiping away a late tear.

'These men, these names, they are not abstract reputations. They are real people, our personal friends. They have lived with us, often in our houses, sometimes for years. Donatello spent months at a time in a shed in our garden while the Palazzo Medici was being built. Sandro Botticelli lived with us in the house, sharing our food, for two years. He and Lorenzo have been close friends since they were boys. And Leonardo da Vinci, and Poliziano ...'

'Stop! Please stop.' His hand was raised over his head in defence, as if he expected a beating.

She stiffened, surprised and confused at the sudden outburst.

He shook his fists, as if surrounded by invisible demons, batting them away with his hands. 'They are all the same. Don't you realize? All of them ...'

'What?' She could see his fear and distaste but did not understand the reason for it.

'As my German friends in the University of Bologna used to say, *Florenzers*. Sodomites, every one.'

She shook her head. 'You must not believe everything you hear. If you are rich and famous there are always people who want to drag you down. And what is the easiest accusation to make?' She shrugged.

'Are you trying to tell me it isn't true? Is this, then, another of those layers of the onion that have to be peeled away?' He looked as if he wanted to believe her, but there was no doubt about the concern on his face.

Lucrezia found herself short of breath. It was a question she and Piero had discussed many times, especially when Lorenzo was young and so in thrall to Sandro Botticelli and Angelo Poliziano. And under their roof too. This was by no means the first time she had wondered exactly what membership of the Platonic Academy had come to involve by the time Lorenzo became an active participant.

But this was no time to dig up old bones. She forced herself to smile. 'There is, no doubt, some element of truth in every statement. But also gross exaggeration.' She tried to make her voice sound light, as she had done in the past when her children were young and frightened. 'We are talking about boys experimenting, playing silly games, learning by trying and by doing what is right and wrong. But I do not believe any young man in Florence is ... at risk.' She shook her head again. 'It simply isn't true.'

But even as she gave the assurance, she remembered conversations with Piero, and even more with Giovanni, who was always so much easier to talk to, especially in matters concerning life. Perhaps to convince herself, she decided to tell Savonarola a story.

~

PALAZZO MEDICI
November 1467

'We cannot allow matters to continue like this. I cannot believe the accusations have a single element of truth in them. Nevertheless, everyone is gossiping and if we leave it, matters will only get worse.'

Lucrezia nods absent-mindedly. The problem is that even at seventeen she is pretty sure Lorenzo will run rings around his father. Especially on a matter that embarrasses Piero much more than it embarrasses her son. But despite her reservations about how to handle Lorenzo, Lucrezia has to agree. Something has to be done and, in theory at least, Piero, as head of the household, is the one to do it.

Piero calls Lorenzo to him the following day. 'There are unkind rumours coming from the *Mercato Vecchio*.'

Lorenzo nods, disinterested. 'Yeah. Always. You wouldn't believe what goes on up there at night. Frightens my horses it does.' He smirks and waits for the next move.

'They say you go to the marketplace at night.'

'Course I do. We all do. That's where the fun is. I'm seventeen, Father. You can't expect me to sit at home and play the lute. There's a life out there and I'm going to live it while I can.'

'What do you mean while you can?'

'Well, once I'm married I'll have to be a bit more circumspect, won't I? But at the moment, the fun's all to be had at the *Mercato Vecchio*.'

'What do you do there all night?'

'You know. Dress up. Show off our new clothes. Strut about with our best falcons. Race the greyhounds. Lay trails for the scent-hounds. Race our horses.'

'Play football?' Piero is trying to show he understands.

'Football? At my age? Have a heart. I haven't played football for three years. Too much risk of getting clattered.'

'Clattered? What does that mean?'

'You know. Kicked, barged into the crowd, tripped so you fall into a horse trough. They all picked on me in my last few games. I was targeted. Everyone wanted to be the one that clattered Lorenzo. So I quit.'

'I wish you wouldn't use that modern language. It's coarse.'

'It's Tuscan. The language of our people.' Predictably, Lorenzo has become combative.

'I know, and Dante and Petrarch and Boccaccio …'

'You know, so why ask me?'

Lucrezia, sitting quietly in the corner, shoots a glance at Piero, who realizes he's been led off the trail. She jerks her head to tell him to get back to the point.

Piero does his best. 'They say all sorts of immoral things are going on up there.'

Lorenzo grins. 'I'll say. Short measures on silk. Over-pricing of olive oil. Clipped coins. And, of course, usury. They all say the bankers are the worst when it comes to breaking the law.'

Piero looks at Lucrezia and shrugs his impotence.

She takes a deep breath and launches into it. 'They say you are having sex with men.' Her voice is clipped. The voice Lorenzo knows not to joke with.

But Lorenzo is prepared, and doesn't bat an eyelid. 'Who in particular?'

She swallows hard, embarrassed, but committed now. 'They say you are having sex with Sandro.'

Lorenzo laughs aloud. 'I would hardly need to drag myself all the way to the marketplace to have sex with Sandro, would I? He lives here, under the same roof.'

'Answer the question.' Piero is losing his temper now. Not a common occurrence, but nasty when it happens.

'Oh really? I'm supposed to be having sex with Sandro, am I? And who is supposed to be fucking who?' Lorenzo has a tendency to coarsen the conversation when he is defending himself. He knows his parents don't like it and it puts them off their stride.

Of course, Piero has not considered that sort of unpleasant detail, but as Sandro is four years older than Lorenzo, he assumes he is the perpetrator, and so he answers accordingly.

Lorenzo just laughs and says, 'Out of the question.' As he walks out of the door, he stops, turns and shakes his head. 'I don't do submissive.'

~

Lucrezia gave Girolamo her most motherly smile. 'And of course that was the end of that.'

But even as she uttered the words, she found herself hearing them in a new way. Originally, when Lorenzo had made his response, she had accepted it as he presented it; as a simple denial of a scurrilous allegation. But now, in talking to this monk and in deciding what to say and what to omit, she began looking at her family with a different eye, from outside. And this time, it had to be said, with the awareness of Lorenzo's slippery facility with words.

Now she was uncertain. Had her son's denial been nothing of the sort but rather a lawyer's sidestep, redefining the question in such a way as to enable denial?

Now, uncomfortably, she found herself unsure. Of course Lorenzo didn't play the submissive. It would have been out of character. Lorenzo always dominated any relationship with another person, man or woman. All relationships were, to him, comparisons, measures of greatness, contests. And as contests, he had to win every one of them. No, Lorenzo would never put himself in any position that even hinted at passivity, never mind submission. She was sure of that.

Besides, he would have had no need to. The richest, most glamorous, charming, brilliant and powerful man in Florence had never needed to. Lorenzo, she knew with certainty, was never the seeker, but always the sought. They all pursued him. Of course they did. They pursued him for his money and for his patronage and for his influence. Simply to be able to say 'I am a friend of Lorenzo' was to open doors, to wealth, power and opportunity. She had always accepted that. But never, until this moment, had she questioned the extent or nature that their pursuit might take. It would certainly never have reflected pursuit in the sense of dominance.

But the reverse? The reverse might well be true. Women pursued men ruthlessly on occasions, but always by carefully controlled retreat. The thrill of the chase, by offered, or perhaps better by subtly suggested, submission.

A cold shiver ran through her as she heard them again, echoes after all these years. Especially Angelo Poliziano, with his courtly mock-grovelling. 'I bow to your pleasure,' he'd say to Lorenzo. And Lorenzo? Now she looked back, she remembered how he would always snigger, as if it was a private joke. Well, private, but perhaps, less of a joke than she had always assumed.

Unnerved, she looked at her companion and realized that her comfortable assurances had failed to convince him too. They continued their walk awkwardly; he looking at her with suspicious uncertainty while she wished she had not tried to overcome his concerns quite so blandly.

'Our friendship with the artists was not always a simple source of pleasure to us.'

They had walked half-a-mile in silence and Lucrezia had been trying to think of a way to retrieve matters after her mistake.

Beside her, perhaps for the same reason, Savonarola was generous, and tipped his head to one side in apparent interest. 'Why was that?'

'No. Sometimes they became involved in other aspects of our life. I remember just over two years after Cosimo had died, Andrea Mantegna visited Florence before going on to Pisa, largely, as I remember it, to see the engraving and printmaking skills of Francesco Rosselli, who, of course, we knew through Sandro, who was his close friend.

'He had painted a portrait of Carlo as a cardinal, and he brought it for us to see. It was a good likeness, very good. Carlo hadn't changed. He still had his mother's colouring and his father's features, the long nose and the big, elephantine ears. Although now, as he got older, his eyes had begun to droop just like Cosimo's. It gave him a baleful look, although Andrea said he had been in quite good spirits while he was being painted.

'The conversation reminded me of the last time I had spoken to Carlo, at Cosimo's funeral, when he told me of his mother's death. Somehow, seeing his face again spurred me into action and I wrote to the abbess the next day. Just a short note, in general terms, but making reference to Maddalena and saying how much I regretted the fact and the manner of her departure from his life.

'It wasn't all that long after receiving her reply that we were told Donatello had died. His funeral at San Lorenzo was attended by everybody – nobility and great painters. Mantegna was there, on his way back home from Pisa and this time he had Carlo with him.

'The abbess's letter contained a surprise. She referred to Maddalena as being in the convent "as part of the great one's secret plan for his grandson", and she said she thought I should know all about it. Of course, I assumed she meant Lorenzo, and as his mother, I was, to say the least, intrigued.

'With Piero still alive although increasingly unwell, I had not really felt empowered to take the matter further, and I could hardly say anything to Carlo, who, I was sure, was not part of the plan. But the abbess's letter had referred to Donatello "bringing information that had been a great comfort to *Suora* Maddalena", so I knew he had been involved, somehow.

'I had promised myself for some time that I would find a way to talk to him about it, but he had been living out his old age in a small farm, on the Cafaggiolo estate, and somehow the opportunity to go there quietly and unobserved had never arisen. Now, suddenly, he was dead. Time was running out and I began to wonder whether I should visit the convent before the abbess too died and Cosimo's great secret, whatever it was, disappeared forever.'

They reached the top of the steep path back down to the Bagno and she smiled at her companion. 'Remind me to tell you all about it, some time.'

Chapter 9
Doing too Much

'Giovanni?' Giovanni di Pace put his head round the door. 'Can you take a message to the monk, please? Tell him I cannot walk with him today. I am too weary for that steep path. The doctor says I must rest.'

He nodded. 'He's already outside, waiting, Mona Lucrezia. Shall I send him away?'

She sighed, considered, and then shook her head. 'No. In that case, can you tell him I will join him in ten minutes, at the top pool? Giovanni departed, still nodding. 'Oh and Giovanni?' His head reappeared. 'Can you clear everyone away from the upper pool, please, and make sure we have privacy for the rest of the morning? Thank you.'

Lucrezia opened her closet and began looking for a clean cotton *camicia* and her embroidered sleeveless *cotta* – the cream damask one, brocaded with the green silk embroidery – to wear over it. If it got too hot she could slide into the pool in those and absorb the minerals while they were talking. And with that embroidery around the bust she hoped she wouldn't look too brazen. *It's not the young monk's eyes that concern me, but I'm not as firm as I once was.*

He was already waiting when she reached the pool. He looked solicitous, perhaps also disappointed that the previous day's conversation had slid astray and never really recovered itself. 'I am sorry to hear that you are unwell.'

She sat beside the pool and immersed her feet and ankles. The water had an immediate chill but then, even before she had time to change her mind, it became refreshing and she left them where they were. She remembered the discussion that had gone into the building of that pool. A natural grotto shaped like a steep amphitheatre, curved in a natural rock semi-circle taller than a man's head, of clean, yellow rock – quite distinct amongst the grey metalliferous rocks of the volcanic mountains around them.

A small natural waterfall already spilled over the edge of the cliff and they had piped it across so that it fell exactly in the centre and then they had hewed out the rock below to produce a deep pool below the waterfall, shallowing gently toward the edges, and with a single narrow runnel to allow the excess water to escape and spill down into the next pool, a much larger one further down the valley and some twenty feet below where she now sat.

'Thank you for your concern. It's nothing serious.'

She watched as he walked across to the small plunge pool close underneath the rock face and removed his sandals. His feet, as always, were filthy and carefully he washed them before padding back across the smooth rock and sitting opposite her with the heels of his feet just immersed in the edge of the water.

'You have been doing too much.' His face was kindly and concerned, and she began to relax. After the previous day she had expected criticism.

'That's what my doctor says.' She smiled, leaning back on her elbows, swishing her feet from side to side.

'Is it a habit you have? Doing too much?'

At first, she thought of denying it, but then she spotted an opportunity. 'A reaction.'

His eyebrows furrowed. 'To what? Or perhaps I should say against what?'

'Initially against imprisonment. And later ...' she smiled at the memory, 'against release.'

He smiled back at her. Perhaps he realized that she was teasing him. 'I don't understand.'

She sat upright and turned to her left, leaning on an elbow. 'Why do men not take women seriously? Why do they not treat them as equals?'

She could see he was interested but he would not be drawn. He shook his head. 'Tell me why.'

'Because, in the main, women are not educated. Because they have access neither to the knowledge that underlies interesting conversation, nor the language and the rhetorical skills with which to explore its opportunities. And as a result, men –

educated men – find their conversation boring.'

'But you have all those things. They do not, surely, find you boring?'

Lucrezia looked at the expression on his face. Was it solicitous or just simpering? He probably thought she was fishing for compliments. She made sure her reply proved him wrong because she was deadly serious.

'I am different. My father ensured that I had a complete and equal humanist education. I was taught Latin and Greek, Rhetoric and Logic from an early age. Instead of embroidery, I studied finance and banking practice and although I studied music, I was also taught how to keep accounts and the skills of market negotiation. As a child I read Ovid, Cicero and Plutarch. I can read the *Libro Segreto* of the Medici Bank and I understand its subtleties. I write and publish poetry and I own and manage a number of successful businesses in my own name, including this one.'

He nodded. 'I'm impressed.'

Now she was sure he thought she was bragging. But she could also see a question in his face, perhaps because he did not know why she was doing so. All to the good. It was that interest she needed to encourage if she was to achieve her objective. But there was no rush. *All in good time.*

'I was brought up with the younger Medici boys, in the Palazzo Medici. I played with them, read with them, rode with them, with Giovanni and Carlo and with my brother Giovanni Battista. Giovanni was the eldest of our group and he was our leader and our champion – fearless, courageous, charming, amusing and inspiring. So I know the Medici, I know how they work, how they play, how they fight and how they think.'

'Surely, then, a world of opportunity.'

'You would think so, wouldn't you?'She shook her head. 'Unless someone is stupid enough to marry you to P-P-P-Piero.'

'Your husband didn't treat you as an equal?'

This time she snorted in derision. 'Equal? I didn't want to be his equal. I was a lot more than his equal. The harsh truth is that Piero was a man of very limited ability, very little imagination, and absolutely no charm whatsoever. His perceptions, his expectations and his aspirations were all limited to the point of invisibility.' She pointed to her own chest. 'I was a modern woman and he held me back!'

He looked at her and opened his mouth but finally did not reply. For a moment it looked as if he was afraid to.

'I used to go to the Mercato Vecchio and see the caged birds there, finches and canaries. I used to buy them all and let them go.'

'Because Piero kept you caged?'

She nodded, shaking at the memory. 'He tried. He tried to hold me down.'

'Jealousy?'

She shook her head. 'Worse than that. He didn't have the brains to be jealous. He was simply copying what he had seen his father do with Contessina.' She shook her head again, this time more slowly but with more feeling. 'Sadly Piero had inherited his limited talents from his mother. Like her he was a magpie, collected things and sat and looked at them as if the wealth that had bought them was some measure of his success.' She snorted, dismissively. 'No doubt, given a chance, he would have proved adept at embroidering table cloths as well.'

'So he held you back?'

'He tried. And his dim-witted mother tried to help him. But I learned to escape. It was making me ill, so I began to take the cure, first at Macerato then at Spedaletto to the north, beyond Volterra, and then here, at Morba. And quietly I began to build a world of my own. I had inherited a couple of shops in Pisa, which paid a pittance in rent, so when the tenancies came to an end, I didn't renew but instead put managers in and ran the businesses myself, with Francesco the Goldsmith acting as my local factor.' Suddenly, she laughed, defiantly. 'We finished up with two whole streets and a hotel at one end. And by then I also had my own account with the Monte Ordinario.'

She saw his blank expression. 'You don't have those on Ferrara? The Monte are Tuscan savings banks run by the various cities and communes as a way of raising funds. You buy shares for a fixed period of years and at the end you receive your reward – a greater sum. The Monte Commune is for general savings and the Monte delle Doti is specifically for saving enough money for your daughter's dowry.'

His eyes suddenly narrowed. 'You receive interest on your money?'

She waved him away, irritated at her tactical mistake. 'No. Of course not. That would be usury. It's an exchange fee – it's all quite legal and every city has one.'

Across the pool she could see Savonarola make a mental note. He was taking this confessional business more seriously than she had expected and she knew he had marked it down as a point against her.

'He tried to do the same to Lorenzo, to hold him back.' Lucrezia was keen to take his mind off the subject of usury. It was an unnecessary diversion and if she was not careful it would ruin another day. The monk could be such a dogmatist at times.

'I once heard him say: "I am determined that the gosling shall not lead the gander to water." That was the extent to which my husband felt overshadowed by his own son. So he tried to hold him back.'

The tactic worked. Savonarola lifted his head. 'Hold him back? Lorenzo? That would be difficult, surely?'

She nodded, inwardly relieved. 'It was a question of Lorenzo's future wife. Piero had been in negotiations for some time with the Orsini family in Rome. I think my brother, who was running the Rome branch, had convinced him that the future of the bank lay with the Curia branch and that he should strengthen the Medici ties with one of the powerful Roman families.

'At the same time, Piero, in his silly inflated way, had got the idea in his head that it would be a good idea to demonstrate that the Medici were now players in a national game and not just limited to the city and commune of Florence. It was, of course, true, but cocking a snook at the other powerful families in Florence really was crass stupidity. I told him so, but once Piero had made his mind up …' She paused, distracted by the thought, and absent-mindedly chewed the end of a finger-nail. Then, as rapidly as she had lost her train of thought, she re-found it. 'Anyway. I was sent to Rome to have a look at this girl.' Once again, she shook her head. 'As soon as I saw her I was appalled. Breeding nobles is a bit like breeding pigs. If you keep using the same boar, the young become deformed. Everybody knows that but the Orsini seemed to have forgotten.'

She looked up. There was no doubt, she had Savonarola's attention now. He was sitting across the pool with his mouth open.

'The girl sat, as if without stimulus or awareness of her surroundings. Her eyes were dull and lifeless, her mouth half-open, and her shoulders were slouched. I have seen carp with sharper wits.'

She tipped her head from side to side. 'On reflection, that slouched manner of sitting may have reflected her embarrassment at having a very flat chest. The poor girl had not really finished growing. I didn't want to be unfair but compared with our girls, by which I mean all three, Maria, Nannina and Bianca Maria, she was a nonentity. I felt I was in a very difficult position. There was no doubt that Piero had made considerable progress in his discussions with the girl's father and I wasn't clear whether we were already too far committed to withdraw. So I wrote a very careful letter to Piero expressing my reservations, but trying to be supportive at the same time.'

She looked away as she spoke, hearing the voice in her head. *Don't tell him the real reason why you did not reject the girl.*

She had seen the report the Night Watch in Florence had submitted to Piero and she shared his concerns. That's why she had been willing to go to Rome in the first place because, like Piero, she thought her son was out of control and with anyone other than a shy dimwit as his wife, all hell might break loose.

The letter had come at the most delicate time, with Lorenzo's marriage (thankfully by proxy at this stage) only weeks away. She remembered the letter all too well. Even now, she could repeat it, almost verbatim.

~

PALAZZO MEDICI
January 1469

Piero reads the letter, his expression darkening with every sentence. At the end he looks up.

'Well? What does it say?'

Speechless, his hand shaking, he hands it over to her:

To the Magnificent Piero de' Medici, greetings.

We write to you on a matter of the greatest sensitivity. You will be aware that certain young men, especially members of your son Lorenzo's brigata, are wont to sit at night upon the benches on the north side of the Mercato Vecchio and specifically on either side of the steps leading to the loggia above the fattoria of one Felippe Vaiai of the Guild of Furriers and Skinners.

It is their practice to dress lewdly, in tight giornea and groin-hugging hose, showing off their falcons and their running dogs and making shameful remarks to the "pretty-boys" and sodomites who infect that area at night.

It has now come to our attention that many of the brigata have been seen ascending the steps to the loggia above where they are said by reliable witnesses to be performing acts of gross indecency with one another, and, moreover, bragging of their exploits by returning to the street with their clothing still half-open.

We write to you to avoid the embarrassment that persons known to you may in the near future find themselves arrested by the night patrol on charges of gross indecency.

The Night Watch … (Signatures illegible)

She finishes the letter and looks at her husband. 'What shall we do?'

'We must hold him back. The family name will be ruined. I shall talk to him in the sternest possible terms.'

Lucrezia's heart sinks. Already she can hear Piero's attempts at being s-s-stern and Lorenzo's muffled sniggers.

~

It had, as expected, been a disastrous conversation. Lorenzo had won easily, Piero finally walking out of the room in exasperation, his footsteps followed by his son's laughter.

Her own approach at the time had been simpler. She had waited until Piero was bedridden with one of his attacks of gout and then she had showed the letter to Lorenzo. 'Listen to me. If you are ever caught, I shall have all of your falcons strangled in their hoods and Il Morello castrated. That's a promise.'

And for a time, it had worked. Lorenzo loved his friends, but in truth he loved his falcons and his favourite racehorse even better.

'But the marriage went ahead?' Savonarola looked at her, confused, no doubt wondering why she had stopped speaking.

'What? Oh yes. Piero had made the decision and as a dutiful wife I had to support him. I had other tasks to perform while I was in Rome. I performed the diplomatic mission that Piero had entrusted me with, a sensitive conversation with the pope, and then I prepared to come home. Just as I was about to leave Rome I went down with a heavy cold and took days to recover. Still, I must have set off before I was fully strong again, because by the time we reached Assisi ...'

Savonarola began shaking his head. 'I don't understand. You came from Rome to Florence via Assisi? Why Assisi?'

She raised a hand, irritated that he should intrude on a matter that did not concern him. 'I had business there, on behalf of the pope. I came on to Fuligno by the beginning of May and there I was taken very ill with bronchitis. Luckily I was treated by Maestro Girolamo. Without him, I think I might have died.'

'You were travelling alone? Surely not?'

Still irritated, she shook her head. 'Of course not. I was accompanied by Filippo Martelli, by two of my brothers, Leonardo and Niccolò, and by Bartolomeo, a valiant constable with all his men. But it was Maestro Girolamo who saved my life. Finally we came by way of Arezzo and I broke the news of the marriage arrangements to Lorenzo when I reached home.'

'How did he take it?'

'He seemed irritated and disinterested.' The image of the

Night Watch letter leapt into her head again.She shook her head, concentrated, and forced a smile. 'Lorenzo had already become infatuated with Lucrezia Donati, to the point where he had given up his liaisons with two others he had in tow that summer. I think they were called Elena and Matilda. So it was hard to get him to concentrate on his marital responsibilities. He kept questioning me on what she was like and he must have read my hesitancy. Finally, resorting to coarseness as he sometimes did when he was trying to shock me, he said, "has she got any tits?"

'I said, "she's from a very noble Roman family," and he said, "Oh. No tits at all, then."' She looked up. 'All in all it wasn't a very productive conversation.'

'But you had recovered from your illness?' Savonarola seemed to have lost the train of her argument, which was not surprising, as in her attempts to lead him off the trail of usury she had almost lost it herself.

'Temporarily, yes. The bronchitis went but I was left with indigestion and depression. A black mood came over me and hung on for all that summer.'

'Did you know why?'

'Not at the time, but looking back now it all seems clearer. I think, like Lorenzo, I was just exhausted. In my attempts to break out from the cage that Piero had locked me in, I was simply trying to do too much. And then, as Piero became more and more ill, and less and less effective, I was trying to keep the momentum going and doing as many of his jobs as I could.'

She sat up and stared at Savonarola in emphasis. 'I was trying to be supportive.'

'Although the direction you were pushing things in was, perhaps, not the direction he would have pursued himself?' There was a cynical smile on his face now.

For a moment she was silent, caught out by his perceptiveness. She had thought she had covered that matter better. 'I had to do what I thought was right.'

'For Piero? Or for Lorenzo?'

It was the critical question and she knew she had to answer it truly, because in the end, everything hinged on that one question.

'For the future. For Lorenzo. Piero was part of the past.' She looked into his eyes, hoping he would not judge her too harshly. 'In my mind, Piero, my husband, was already dead.'

He looked at her and said nothing, but his gentle nod seemed to signify that he had understood, and that apparent acceptance encouraged her to continue.

'I was obviously moving too fast. Too fast for Piero, who wanted the world to stay the way it had been in his father's day and perhaps, in view of my succession of illnesses, too fast for me too. And then Lorenzo came out with dreadful eczema, and I realized that in my haste to escape the past, I was probably moving too fast for him as well. And so, in early September, I came here, to the Bagno, and brought Lorenzo with me.'

'And then, finally, with all your tasks completed, you were able to sit and relax?'

She began to laugh. 'Hardly. We had only been here a few days when I received word from Piero. He said he had heard there was a plot to kidnap us both here, at the Bagno. So I sent Lorenzo back to Florence on some excuse. Of course, he expected to return in a few days, but two weeks later he wrote to me. They had talked him round and convinced him to stay in Florence.

'Within days Piero wrote to agree it was safer to keep Lorenzo in Florence, and suddenly I began to realize what was happening. Piero's story about a kidnap had been invented, it had been a ruse to get Lorenzo away from me and back under his own control. Piero, or more likely one of his advisors, must have realized that I was avoiding him and that Lorenzo was taking more notice of me than he was of his father.

'And of course, it was true. I knew I had lost this round in the battle, but I couldn't face returning to Piero and his sick bed, so I stayed here and kept sending letters saying I was too unwell to return. Piero sent Benedictus Reguardati, a very notable physician, to examine me, and he wrote back to Lorenzo almost immediately.

'He described my symptoms accurately. First, pain in the breast, on the left hand side, and up into the shoulder. Secondly, pains in the stomach and spleen, which had been lasting for days, but which, after his potions, were reduced to little over an hour. And finally, a very painful form of sciatica, in the right thigh.

'Over the next four weeks, with a combination of bathing, rest and the physician's potions, I slowly recovered and in the middle of November, having received many solicitous letters from my family, I finally felt well enough to return to Florence.'

'And the marriage between Lorenzo and Clarice Orsini went ahead?'

'Of course. The paperwork was completed and the dowry transferred by early February of 1469 and she and Lorenzo were married by proxy with his cousin, Filippo de Medici, Archbishop of Pisa, acting for him, in Rome.

'She finally came to Florence in June and we celebrated the marriage over three days of memorable entertainment at the Palazzo Medici.'

'With Lorenzo finally, sitting with his bride at his side?' Savonarola seemed to want assurances on everything.

'Well, almost. For most of the time Clarice sat with her silly, giggly friends from Rome and Lorenzo sat elsewhere and entertained his guests – the old *brigata* of course, still ostentatiously carrying a standard given to him by his old girlfriend, Lucrezia Donati.'

'He hadn't forgotten her then?'

Lucrezia shook her head.' No. Not at all. Lorenzo always stuck by his friends. Even years later he was still writing poetry to her, although by then she was married too.'

'So the Medici marriage was not an expression of true love?'

She shook her head. 'I told you. Judge us by what we do, not by what we say. As for the marriage, it was about one thing and one thing only: *parentado* – the importance of linking powerful families together through interlocking marriages. Lorenzo and Clarice didn't pretend to love each other and they still don't.'

Sensing that she had finished, Savonarola rose to his feet and walked over to his sandals. He slid his feet into them and turned toward Lucrezia, who had rolled onto her elbow to watch him. 'It sounds like a very difficult life. One in which you have to be tough to keep your health and sanity.'

She shrugged the one shoulder that could move and stuck out her lower lip in resignation. 'It's about survival. You play the cards you are dealt. That's what women have always had to do.'

Chapter 10
Alas, Poor Piero

It was raining outside. Warm rain with a heavy scent of damp earth and moist young plants. Not heavy rain, more in the nature of heavy mist, but nevertheless wet enough to be a distraction and an irritant.

She had wanted to return to the poolside but he had pleaded embarrassment. 'I recognize that this rain makes no difference to you. Your clothing is intended to become wet. But I have only one habit. What do I wear for our conversations if that becomes soaking wet?'

Finally she had given in to him. She was, she recognized, being selfish, using her position of ownership to make everyone pander to her will. It was a habit she had learned during her childhood in the Palazzo Medici, but as she got older, one she was beginning to regret. The young monk was right. It wasn't necessary. They had a comfortable dry room at their disposal, one with a large open window from which, if she wished, she could still look out and enjoy the freshness that the rain had brought that morning.

The wide eaves of the tiled roof above her head gave complete protection from the rain and now she sat, propped on the edge of the windowsill, while he, returning to their original routine, sat in the corner of the room, facing out toward her.

'Did your husband take long to die?'

For an instant his question struck her as crass, insensitive, even coarse. But then she remembered that he was, after all, only picking up a remark of her own, made late in the previous day.

'Was that such an awful thing for me to say yesterday? That in my mind, my husband was already dead? It wasn't just my mind it was in. The vultures were already lined up along the Via Largo, waiting. And to the south I could imagine even more of them, across the Ponte Vecchio, prowling the corridors and grounds of the Palazzo Pitti, plotting, rehearsing, waiting, each of them desperate for news.

'True to form, he kept us all waiting. He hung on painfully and ineffectively for months. By now he couldn't leave the house, hardly left his bed in fact. Just lay there, in pain, confused at what he had done to deserve such an ending and trying desperately in his mind to find some purpose, some justification for his life by which he might be remembered. But the truth was he was a lost cause and he knew it. The servants drooped around, shoulders bowed, pulling what they thought were the appropriate faces, but in truth bored rigid.

'Lorenzo escaped. He announced that the family needed to make a show of courage and confidence for the *popolani* and he took to the streets, to be seen. Not walking but on his charger, the big white one he called Fortuna.

'And while he faced the world, I sat and faced my dying husband. I had, finally, grown sorry for him. No man should be asked to accept that combination of hopelessness, pain and indignity. I learned, watching him in those final days, the importance of dignity to the dying. Self-esteem is, I think, the last door to close before we give up. Once that is gone, there's nothing else to cling on for except, in the very strong, sheer bloody-mindedness.

'So I stayed with him. He had never been consciously unkind to me. He had no more wanted to marry me than I had wanted to marry him, but somehow between us we had made the most of a bad situation. We had always maintained civility towards each other. In fact, to the outside world, we probably looked like a loving couple.

'The really sad thing is that, even as I watched Piero die, I was grieving for his brother, Giovanni. Somehow, in maintaining family decorum, I had never had a chance to grieve for Giovanni at the time when he had died, but now it all spilled out. The respect, the humour, the sheer physical love of life that he brought to every occasion.'

'You loved him, didn't you? Giovanni?'

He did not look at her as he asked the question, perhaps not wanting to appear intrusive. She watched him, knowing he did not need to lift his head, knowing that today her voice would tell him everything he needed to know, with uncomfortable precision.

Finally, she let it come. It had to some time. 'He was the love of my life.'

She leaned back out of the window and breathed deeply, sucking in the fresh, damp air and remembering Giovanni in the garden of the Palazzo Medici, his arm round her shoulder, reciting poetry to her and acting the fool.

'How did you cope?'

She turned, looking out at the gardens below, picking her words carefully. 'It wasn't always easy. As I told you yesterday, I threw all my energies into Lorenzo. For years I had known he was the future ...' She paused, still looking out of the window, trying to decide whether or not to go down the path that had just opened up in her mind. And finally made a decision. 'As had Cosimo.'

She looked across the room at Savonarola and wondered whether he remembered. His expression answered her question immediately.

'He made ... provision for his grandson, you told me. On his deathbed?'

She saw him look up, sharply, and she nodded. 'Yes. His investment in the future, he called it. Lorenzo's Gold.'

Again she looked out of the window, thinking, deciding, filtering. She was about to open a door, a door to a world of secrets, but how wide she should open it she was still undecided. For the benefit of her soul she knew she must tell the truth. She was, after all, in confessional now. But all of it? The risks were high. *If this man broke the secrecy of the confessional, Lorenzo would never forgive me.*

'I knew Cosimo had made provision, but I did not know how much or in what manner. That secret, as he himself had told me, had been taken by Donatello and given to Maddalena at the Convento di Santo Damiano. Now both were dead and the trail had grown cold. There was only one other person who might be able to point me in the right direction.

'The abbess?'

She found herself smiling. 'You *have* been listening.' She saw him grin in return, with what looked like a mixture of pride and apology.

'The abbess, yes. I wrote to her. She replied quickly, sounding relieved, as if she had been finding the responsibility of her secret a heavy burden. She confirmed that everything was there, the first instalment, as she called it, and, amongst Maddalena's few possessions, her journal and her collection of letters from Cosimo. Amongst those, she told me, was his final letter, the one Donatello had brought with him and explained, the one that contained the poem.'

'There was a poem?' The surprise on his face made him sit up sharply.

Lucrezia stood up from her windowsill and walked to the centre of the room. She composed herself, remembering. She must get it right or the whole effect would be ruined. Carefully, from memory, she recited it:

Beneath the goldsmith's secret
Possession, lover, son
There lies the stone of destiny
Whose answer is but one
Ten quarrels equidistant
From where that once we lay
My final diminution
Holds Lorenzo's destiny

She reached the end without hesitation and to her satisfaction he responded. 'Oh well done! You remembered it.'

She returned to her windowsill. 'I am a poet. I do not forget poetry. Not even simple rhymes.

'With Piero on his deathbed it no longer seemed disloyal to visit the abbess. Lorenzo and I made the journey a couple of weeks later. We were supposed to be disguised, but I am sure a number of people recognized us. Everyone knew what Lorenzo looked like, and in any event, he made no secret of his identity

111

once we were amongst the nuns. We took presents, as was customary, mainly food, wine and oil – two cartloads – but also a few books for the library that Cosimo had originally founded.

'Madonna Arcangelica could not have been more welcoming. She insisted on giving us a tour of her convent. It is a fine place and in reasonably good repair, apart from the roof of the main chapel, which had sustained damage during the earthquake.

'She seemed keen to tell her story, especially when she realized that Lorenzo was the very person the whole scheme had been established for. We stood in the chapel, directly beneath the gaping hole where the beams had collapsed, and she pointed to the place where Maddalena had died. They had tidied up and were at that time still using one of the side chapels for their services. They had hung great canvas sheets and some old tapestries to protect it from the worst of the weather. But at the place where Maddalena had been crushed they had left the broken-backed pew as a sort of shrine. It was autumn when we visited and they had a pot of water with branches from the hedgerows covered in wild berries. A simple tribute but one, I thought, fitting.

'She took us to the library and the vault and with due ceremony she gave Lorenzo the keys to the two great chests that were in there. He unlocked them and, to our amazement and satisfaction, we found gold, a great deal of gold, all in brand new florins from Cosimo's time. We had them loaded into our carts and as we were doing so, I lifted my eyes to the damaged roof and signalled to Lorenzo.

'He is such a good boy. He realized instantly what I meant and insisted that two of the great bags – two thousand florins, be given to the abbess to see to the necessary repairs. Afterward, as we were returning home by way of Fiesole, I asked him why he had been so generous. The repairs to the roof could, I knew well, have been done for a quarter of the money – perhaps less. He smiled and said, "She knew that money was there and she knew that nobody else had any idea how much of it there was. But still, even with that hole in the roof a daily reminder, and providing the most perfect of moral excuses, she did not help herself to it.

That is why I rewarded her handsomely." And of course, he was right.

'Afterward we ate together with the nuns, and Lorenzo made a speech. It was a good one, for a change, without any of the lewd jokes he often liked to slide in, and the nuns seemed delighted. Then the abbess presented us with Maddalena's casket, containing her breviary, her bible, her journal and the letters she had received from Cosimo over the years, and we left.

'Lorenzo allowed me to take the casket. "You and Maddalena were always friends," he said. "Besides, you are a better poet than I am. I will leave it to you to decipher my grandfather's message." It was typical of Lorenzo to delegate the onerous tasks, but it was also a kindness, as it gave me something to do while I wiled away the hours as Piero lay dying.

'My husband finally died late on the evening of the first of December. By the time the doctors had pronounced him dead it was past sunset. I'm sure it was a relief for him, as it was for all of us. Nobody grieved. Those who needed to had long done their grieving. We were just content that it was all over and we could stop holding our breath.

'Of course, as you have learned to expect,' she flicked her eyes across the room and saw Savonarola nod, 'protocol took over. For his own good reasons Lorenzo wanted to make his father's death more of a political event than it really was. "My father is dead, grieve with me" had a better ring to it than, "take notice, I am in charge now". So the funeral was made a men-only affair and, as such, political rather than personal, public rather than family.'

'The reverse of Cosimo's funeral, then?'

Savonarola had found a way of sitting with his elbows on the arms of the chair, his hands clasped together, and his chin rested on his thumbs. Although relaxed, he looked very attentive.

She left the window and began walking slowly around the room. 'Exactly. With Cosimo's death we had wanted to play down the vacuum we knew was left behind. But now the story was reversed. This time we wanted everyone to feel safe in the knowledge that Piero could do no more harm and that Lorenzo the Magnificent was …'

'In charge?'

She stopped walking and shook her head. 'In a republic, we could not presume that. No, we simply made it clear that he was now the head of the family, and left it to others to respond.'

She reached the back of her chair and stood with her hands resting on it, facing him. There was a finality to her stance as she remained unspeaking.

Sensing that the conversation was over, he lifted his head from his hands and made to rise from his chair. 'Judge us by what we do?'

She grinned. 'Yes. But as you do so, always ask yourself why we do it.'

Savonarola nodded to himself and she could read his expression. *Oh but I always do. Every day* , it said.
She smiled to herself as she watched him leave.

He's a bright one, this, and learning fast. From now on I shall have to be extra careful how much I say to him.

Chapter 11
To be a Prince

Overnight the mist and rain had blown away and although it was nearly June, the air had the gentle freshness of a spring day. To Girolamo, Madonna Lucrezia looked much improved. The drawn look had gone from her face and for the moment she no longer seemed to wince every time she sat down. *She does seem to be a worrier*, he thought.

Her health had seemed to decline immediately following that mental slip, a few days before, when it was obvious she had found herself trying to defend something she was less than sure about herself. He wondered whether some aspect of his questions that day had pricked her conscience or whether, in answering him, she had for the first time questioned something she had always taken for granted.

But young as he was … *why do people insist on describing me as young? At nearly thirty I am almost middle-aged. Perhaps my relative un-worldliness makes me appear young to the people here?* Young as he was, he did not fall into the trap of assuming that every action in others was a reaction in response to something he had done. It was just as likely (even as he thought about it, the memory of his early lectures in medicine at the University of Ferrara sprung to mind) that it was the beginnings of the onset of her illness, whatever it was, that had caused her to lose her usual focus and clarity and go off like that.

But she did seem to be on the mend now. She had, at least, accepted his suggestion that they walk once again, gently this time, not high into the hills but following their side of the valley through the woods, just above the river with the roar and swirl of the water still audible further below and the smell of still-damp moss and pine trees wrapping itself around them.

'How long did it take you to crack the code?' *No point in beating about the bush.* As he spoke, a pine-marten ran along a branch above them and she looked up, almost flinching away from the unexpected movement.

He was almost ready to ask the question again when she replied. 'The poem? Oh not long. Less than a week, on and off, you know.'

She watched the pine-marten climb higher in the tree and once she knew what it was, smiled at its agility. 'I had hindsight on my side and, looking back, with the specific questions in mind, I remembered seeing things.'

~

GARDEN, PALAZZO MEDICI
23rd January 1470

'Are you talking to yourself again, Mother?'

Lucrezia, standing before the Donatello David in the garden, looks up. Lorenzo is walking towards her, grinning. 'What did you say?'

'I asked if you were talking to yourself.'

'No you didn't. You said *again*. Are you implying that I've fallen into the habit of talking to myself?'

He's still grinning, despite the cold. 'Of course you do. But only quietly. And only when you think you're alone. It's usually your poetry. You practise it, walking round the garden, by yourself.'

'Oh that? Well yes. I have to admit. But it wasn't my poetry I was rehearsing this time, it was your grandfather's.'

She points to the statue. David, looking remarkably like Carlo looked a few years before and also, from certain angles, like Maddalena, stands erect and proud, his left foot on Goliath's severed head, his sword hand resting the great sword point-downward, beside the head.
She begins to recite the poem:

Beneath the goldsmith's secret
Possession, lover, son...

As she speaks, she nods toward the statue.

Lorenzo turns and follows her eyes. Then a great grin spreads across his face. 'Oh you clever old thing! It is, isn't it? That's Donatello's secret: *the goldsmith's secret.*'

He looks at the statue. At one time it represents Cosimo's slave and lover Maddalena, and their son Carlo. *Possession, lover, son.*

There lies the stone of destiny
Whose answer is but one

Now it's Lorenzo's turn to recite. She hadn't realized that he had learned the poem. He must have been listening more intently than he had pretended at the time.

He looks up at her, and then approaches the statue. 'If this is Donatello's secret, then what is meant by *beneath the goldsmith's secret*? There must be something somewhere here? In the plinth?' He begins poking around, working his way slowly round the base, feeling with his fingertips.

It doesn't take long. 'Here, look.' His voice has dropped to a whisper. He has found a crevice and as he picks at it with the tip of his dagger, a small block of stone – hardly more than a sliver – perhaps a thumb's width thick at the most – loosens and allows him to draw it out. The dagger probes the cavity and Lorenzo, now wholly absorbed, gives a triumphant cry. 'Aha. Look what I've found!'

The disc of stone is larger than a florin but smaller than the palm of his hand. It is perfectly round, flat on the bottom and domed above. It is smooth on both sides, but while the bottom is unmarked, the upper side has three marks painted on it: a dot in the centre, a thin line, running through the centre and from one side to the other, and a shorter, thicker line, in line with the central dot and marking the periphery a short distance to the left of the longer line.

Lorenzo lifts it, hefts it in his hand, grins and calls a servant. 'Can you bring me a shallow saucer please? As big as the palm of my hand or a bit larger?'

The servant runs off and soon returns. Lorenzo puts the stone flat-side down in the centre of the saucer and walks across to the little pond at the base of the fountain. He winks at his mother as he floats the saucer.

'*The stone of destiny*. It's a lodestone. I bet it's a lodestone.'

Freed, the saucer begins to turn until the line though the disc points to the centre of the north side of the garden. Lorenzo squats and looks along the line, then moves until he can sight along the shorter line.

'*Whose answer is but one*. Where should it be floated and what does it point to? That's the question.'

Lucrezia began to recite the second half of the poem:

Ten quarrels equidistant
From where that once we lay
My final diminution
Holds Lorenzo's destiny

Lucrezia's mind goes back to the abbess's original description of how Cosimo and Maddalena had come to the convent together and had finally said their last farewells. There had been something coy yet knowledgeable about the way she said it that suggested something known but hidden.

From where, that once, we lay.

'With the pauses emphasized, it takes on a different complexion. Perhaps it refers to the last time they were together? Did the abbess's coy expression mean she believed they had …? Not, surely, in a convent?' But the more she thinks about it, the more she is sure. She asks Lorenzo what he thinks, and as soon as she hints at it he understands.

'Yes. It must be. Naughty old grandfather. I didn't think he had it in him. And Maddalena too!" He sounds really proud of them both.

'Let me see,' he says. He stands facing north with his left eye shut and his right hand held vertically, thumb up. 'Due north of the convent and then,' he rotates his hand to the left, 'west a bit?'

He is standing alone, one eye shut and his hand in front of him. But in his mind he's not in the garden of the Palazzo Medici but standing on the ridge of Monte Senario, facing north.

'That's just by the side of the ridge crest. We had a stag up there last year, close to the ...'

He gets the rest in one flash of inspiration and looks up. 'It's the Badia di Buonsollazzo. Where Cosimino is buried. It's in exactly the right direction. And the distance? *Ten quarrels*. Ten shots with a crossbow. It's about right. It must be. *My final diminution*, that means Cosimino.' He starts to laugh. 'I told you so. It's where Cosimino is buried. *My final diminution*. That's not bad for Grandfather.'

Lucrezia shakes her head. 'But if the gold is buried beneath Cosimino's tomb, how are you going to get it back ... without attracting attention?'

Lorenzo, a mile ahead of her as usual, simply laughs. 'That, mother dear, is the easy part. It will be dead easy.'

He stands, shaking his head and grinning. 'Who would have thought it? All that argument about where we should bury him. And now I know why. Thank you Cosimo. I couldn't have planned it better myself.'

~

Savonarola looked at her and wondered whether, in their previous conversations, she had told him anything about arguments over Cosimino's burial. He didn't remember her saying anything. And usually, he didn't forget much.

She stopped walking and turned toward him on the narrow path. Then she smiled, as if some things were so obvious they didn't require further explanation. And he, seeing he was going to have to ask her, opened his hands in supplication. 'All right. For those of us who are slower on the uptake than your son, how?'

She was by no means a good-looking woman but today he thought Madonna Lucrezia looked five years younger. For days she had been telling him of death, of decline, of the failure of banks, but now she had a story to tell in which she and her son triumphed. And it suited her. The dappled light falling between the trees flickered gently on her face as she enjoyed her moment.

Finally, she spoke. 'Lorenzo had Cosimino re-buried. In San Lorenzo. He and Giuliano commissioned a tomb, nominally for Giovanni and Piero, but they insisted that Cosimino's little body was brought there too. To be united with his father, they said. Verrocchio it was that designed it for them, from drawings created by his new assistant, Leonardo da Vinci. And together they built it.'

She placed a hand on his forearm. 'When you get back to Florence, you must visit the Church of San Lorenzo and see it.' She grinned. 'But don't bother looking for the gold. Somehow it never arrived at the new tomb.'

There was a sigh of wind high in the trees. The weather was changing again. More rain was coming, perhaps overnight. But for the present, they had plenty of time to return to the Bagno à Morba. They started walking again, choosing the right-hand path, to take them back to the beginning of their walk. They reached a clearing in the trees, with a view across the valley and down to the river not far below them.

He paused and looked down at the water. 'Was there a lot?'

Ahead of him, he saw her stop in mid-stride and look back. He waited, still standing, still looking downward. *She heard me. She's just deciding what to tell me.*

'A lot? What of?'

He smiled. *She did say she had been taught market negotiation. When she was younger. She hasn't lost it.*

'Of gold. A lot of gold. Was there a lot of gold under Cosimino's tomb?'

She wrinkled her eyebrows, as if struggling to remember. 'Yes, I think so. Quite a lot.'

Almost absent-mindedly, she turned and began walking away. 'Yes I think there must have been.'

Chapter 12
Rotten to the Core

'Have you ever had toothache? I mean real, painful, won't-go-away toothache, which lasts for days and drives you mad?'

He shook his head. 'God has spared me that discomfort.'

She had, of course, had her way. They had returned to the poolside.

She had woken feeling fully recovered, her self-confidence returned, regrets for recent events thrown behind her. It had been a mistake to set that hare running, about Lorenzo and his friends in the Platonic Academy. She wasn't to know how deeply the young monk had been seared by his experiences in Ferrara. But she couldn't change anything now and they did seem to have moved on without the subject being resurrected. *It's gone. Done. Can't be retrieved. Just forget it and move on.*

And that's what she was doing. The story needed to be brought to a conclusion. There was not that much more to confess, although she had to admit, the process of opening her soul, whilst uncomfortable at the time, had eased something inside her. Even her lumps felt easier.

'Have you *seen* a tooth that has been removed? A rotten one?' He shook his head. 'A rotten tooth is an edifice to falsity, a statue to misrepresentation. The outside remains, a bastion of strength and whiteness, the hardest bone in the human body, so they say. But inside all is decay, corruption and vileness.'

Across the pool, Savonarola sat up, his knees pulled toward him, his arms wrapped around them and his expression suddenly alert and attentive. 'Yes. I understand.'

She noticed that his eyes were glittering with concentration and she realized that something in her words must have caught his attention. *Oh no. I spoke of corruption. He's gone back to his memories of Ferrara. Never mind. It can't be helped. Keep going. The bank. Keep talking about the bank.*

'Unless it is removed, the infection spreads, corrupting all around it, until the whole mouth is infected with the same awful condition. And by then…' She lifted a finger, swirled it briefly in the water before her, then pointed it at him, 'it is too late.'

She saw him smile, a grim, unkind smile, and although she was certain that it was her words that had triggered the thought in his head, there was something – a remoteness to his expression to suggest that the thought, whatever it was, was his and his alone. The look was intense yet far away, smiling yet unkind. It was almost the look of someone who was planning cruelty, and immediately it unnerved her. But she was too far committed to her analogy to change direction now.

'The Medici Bank had become like that. Like a rotten tooth. Decayed and infected at the core, with the infection spreading outward as fast as a mouthful of sores.' Across the pool his eyes looked almost disappointed, but she knew he was still listening. 'It had begun, of course, with the death of Giovanni Benci and the decision to do away with the holding company. It was that decision that allowed the infection to spread …'

'But the infection itself? What was it? ' For a moment he seemed to be losing the analogy.

'Nepotism.' She washed her hands in the pool as if they were soiled and then shook the water off before dabbing her palms dry on the opposite shoulders of her *gamurra*. 'It is possible to be both a banker and a prince, as Cosimo showed us, but to do both successfully, you have to remove your princely crown before you enter the bank premises. Once you start to confuse the two, all is lost.'

'And the Medici Bank had …?'

She nodded. 'And not just Piero, although he seemed to have the capacity for making more mistakes in a day than any other man in creation.'

'No? Not just Piero? Others too?' He seemed to be following, albeit slowly.

'No. Cosimo himself had put quite a few of the wrong people in place before responsibility passed to Piero.'

'Ah yes.' He nodded, seeming to have caught up with her.

'You have told me on a previous occasion about the Milan branch and the developing over-reliance on the Portinari family.'

'Exactly.' She felt an unexpected shiver of concern.

'I also seem to remember the problems in Rome, your husband taking it upon himself to support your brother, Giovanni Battista, against the established management?'

Again Lucrezia felt a little shiver run through her. Such recall. Perhaps what she had read as confusion on his part had merely been guile? Had he been leading her, after all?

A frown wrinkled his forehead. 'But what about Giovanni? Was he not responsible for running the bank for a number of years?'

She shook her head. *You're not going to lay the blame on my Giovanni.* 'The mistakes made during Giovanni's directorship were made by Cosimo. He was always hovering and interfering. Left to his own devices, Giovanni would, I am sure, have sorted the mess out.'

He began to nod his head but extremely slowly, as if he had reservations about what she had told him. 'Yes. If he had really been interested.'

He really has been listening. And remembering what I have told him. This man is not slow; he is careful. He was also thoughtful, in an independent way that she found invigorating and challenging, but at the same time, almost threatening. *Be careful not to over-defend Giovanni.* She shrugged, trying to look relaxed. Not easy to do when you're lying by a shallow pool with your feet in the edge of the water and your weight back on your elbows. 'Giovanni saw the way it was going. He stepped away.'

She rolled onto her right elbow and with her left hand began absent-mindedly flicking small stones into the water. The single large cloud that had thrown its shadow over them for the last fifteen minutes finally moved away and as the brightness of the full sun hit the water between them, she squinted and frowned. *Careful now. Concentrate. Keep the focus on Cosimo. And Sassetti.*

~

PALAZZO MEDICI
14th November 1478

'Forgive me if I seem a little cynical, Francesco, but what I don't understand is why the bank – my bank – is being asked, for the third year running, to pay out a huge bonus to you when all around us I see failure and collapse?'

Francesco Sassetti, general manager of the Medici Bank, squirms in his chair as Lorenzo points his finger at him. Lucrezia sits quietly in the corner. Much as she blames Sassetti for the mess the bank is in, she would not wish Lorenzo's anger upon any man. It even frightens her.

But Sassetti stands his ground. 'Lorenzo, it's merely my entitlement, under the terms of my contract.'

Lorenzo's fist hits the table. 'Your contract as general manager does not tell you to drive the fucking bank into the ground.'

Sassetti flinches, but recovers. 'My contract as general manager tells me to implement the policies of the *Maggiore*. It's them, the majority shareholders, who made the appointments you have been talking about. I didn't appoint any of the Portinari brothers to their positions, nor did I overrule Leonardo Vernacci in Rome in his arguments with your uncle and cause him to leave.'

In the corner Lucrezia squirms at the reference to her brother but says nothing. Lorenzo is in charge and it would be foolish to break his flow. She watches and waits.

Lorenzo raises a hand. 'Never mind Rome. We aren't talking about Rome. We are talking about Milan. Why should I pay you a bonus when this afternoon I need to write to the Milanese Ambassador and break the news that we are closing the Milan branch because it's bankrupt? Because, despite sending cartloads of Sforza jewellery to Venice as collateral against the duke's loans, we can't afford to pay the agreed interest on deposits, including those made by the Bishop of Cuenca.'

Lorenzo looks at his mother, then back to Sassetti. 'Who, I may remind you, is about to receive his cardinal's hat.'

But Sassetti has worked for the Medici for a long time. He's more than capable of keeping his head when a row is brewing. Especially when the outcome involves his own finances. Somehow, over the last twenty years, he's amassed a fortune. 'My bonuses are payable under my partnership agreements in the Avignon and Geneva branches. I receive only a salary as general manager of the Medici Bank.'

'So you look after the interests of those two branches and allow the rest of the bank to go to hell in a hand-basket?' Lorenzo points to his own chest. 'My fucking bank!'

'I'm sorry. But I didn't make the appointments and I didn't write the contracts either. And while we're on the subject, and since you have brought the Geneva branch into the conversation...'

'The so-called Geneva branch, which has actually moved with the trade fairs to Lyon.'

'Yes. The same. Well perhaps I might remind you that although I am a shareholder in that branch, I did not appoint Lionetto Rossi as director of that branch.'

'So what?' There's a vein pulsing on Lorenzo's left temple, always a bad sign.

'Only that Lionetto has recently married your sister, Maria.'

'So what? She's entitled to marry isn't she?'

'It's just that, if my sums are correct, Lionetto in Lyon makes four branches in the hands of men who, being in the family, can't be removed when they fail. And as general manager, in name only, it seems, these days, I just thought I'd point that out.'

~

Lucrezia lifted her eyes across the pool and looked at the monk. 'So at the very time when the bank was heading for disaster, Sassetti's personal fortune was growing hand-over-fist. And my husband finished up presiding over a bank that was losing money and at the same time having to watch it pay out huge bonuses to the general manager.' She shook her head, 'The processes of collapse may have made themselves visible during his period of control, but the origins of those processes went very much further back.'

Savonarola nodded, accepting the precision of what she said, but did not let her off the hook completely. 'Did those origins also precede your brother-in-law's period of office?'

Despite her reclined position, Lucrezia managed to raise her head. She glared at him down the length of her characterful nose. 'Completely. I can assure you that Giovanni remained blameless in all of this. Absolutely blameless.'

All this time Lucrezia had been lounging beside the shallow pool and Girolamo Savonarola had been sitting opposite her, his feet occasionally paddling in the very edge of the water. But now, to his surprise and considerable interest, Mona Lucrezia gave up all pretence of lying beside the medicinal pool and relaxing. Now, instead, she stood up and began marching up and down.

And as she continued to speak, her tone became more hectoring while he, the monk, still sat across the pool, close up against the steep cliff-face and listened. And absorbed. And thought. And learned.

And the lessons she thought she was teaching him about the bank were going in and they were being assimilated with the other half-formed theories he had brought with him when he set out walking in pursuit of this woman. And out of them, slowly, a picture was emerging.

But it was not a picture about the Medici Bank. Like her, he had written that off already as being on the path of self-destruction, and all this talk of rotten teeth had merely served to reinforce his decision. No, the rotten teeth taking shape in his mind were a rich family by the name of Medici and a cynical, corrupt city called Florence. For the lady, in her clarity of exposition, had exceeded all his expectations and the picture he was forming of her family and her city was clearer, and a great deal worse, than he had ever expected.

She was off again now, waving her arms in frustration.

'So I said to Lorenzo, "Don't pour your new-found money into that deep well. And if you're thinking of trying to turn the bank round and make it profitable again, forget it. The bank is fundamentally flawed and although your father and your uncle have both allowed matters to get much worse, the rot set in with Grandfather Cosimo. So don't feel bad about it."'

'Is that what you told him?' He was leading her now. Egging her on while he knew she had her temper raised and was likely to speak more openly than she had done in most of their previous conversations. And more openly than he knew she intended.

'Indeed I did. I did not beat about the bush. And I also told him a few home truths about the political process he faced. "Remember this," I said. "Democracy the way Florence designed it is unworkable, unless there is a rich man stupid enough to keep bailing it out."'

'And what did he say to that?'

'He said, "Cosimo managed it didn't he?" And I said, "Cosimo tried to manipulate the democratic process to allow him to serve his community without losing all his money. And what did they do to thank him? They tried to finish him off more than once. Exile and attempted murder. That's the thanks he got." I told him. "It's the resentment of smaller men, Lorenzo, that's what it is."'

'Did he agree?' By this time, Savonarola's fingers were itching for want of a pen and paper. He was concentrating hard. He must remember this, exactly if he could. He was sure it was going to be important.

'He had no choice but to agree. "Look what happened to your father with Pitti and the Party of the Hill" I reminded him. "It's not over, you know."'

By this time, she was pacing up and down, up and down and turning so fast in her bare feet that he was sure she was going to give herself blisters. But she was also giving him gold and he had no intention of breaking her train of thought.

'I made it clear to him. "Now, for the moment, we have the lid on and tightly screwed down, but it won't last. So my advice to you is to be a prince – be an open prince and to make the people love you for it." That's what I told him.'

He nodded, making mental notes as hard as he could.

'"Oh and make sure it is they who pay for everything, not you." I told him that as well.'

'And did he take your advice?'

'This time he did. I had told him all these things before but Lorenzo, being Lorenzo, needed to work them out for himself. But by now he was ready. This time Lorenzo was delighted to receive the advice he wanted, as I had known he would be. He waited until I had finished and then he said "Once I have taken out all the money I can, they can chuck the bank into the Arno for all I care. I am going to be a great prince."'

For the first time, she stopped pacing and stood next to him, so that he had to squint against the strong sun as he looked up at her. 'And I said, "Lorenzo, you already are."'

'And how did he reply to that?'

Lucrezia's face broke into a broad smile. 'My Lorenzo? Why, he gave a great laugh and he said, "Yes I am, aren't I?"

Chapter 13
Magnificentia

This time, Lucrezia had decided to let him win.

She had been amused when, perhaps conscious of having been on the receiving end of her lecture the previous day, he had come to her early with two stout sticks in his hand and had dared her to walk. And she, being competitive and, as he had rightly surmised, ready once again to escape from the confines of the Bagno, had taken one of the sticks, pointed to the upper path, curving up above the one they had taken days before, and they had set off.

For an hour they climbed, she taking short steps and using her stick, he loping along beside her with the easy energy of youth. They had reached a promontory, a large flat rock with a second rock behind it and slightly higher forming a hard but level bench, and, feeling she had earned a rest, she leaned back and sat, feeling her breath recover and her heartbeat subside as it did so.

Now she felt fully recovered.

In front of them the broad sweep of a bend in the river gave an open vista, trees below them, packed tightly into the valley sides, but up here, where the slope began to ease and the valley opened out, the trees began to thin, giving way to scrub and rocks, purple and sage except for the line of an ochre path falling gently down the hillside opposite, leading back to the bridge below the Bagno.

The shrill cry of an eagle caught her attention and she turned to see it glide, seemingly without effort, all the way down the valley, covering the distance they had just walked in a matter of minutes before turning into the column of warm air she knew was rising in front of the big yellow cliff opposite them. Then she watched as in three leisurely spirals it regained its height and began the easy traverse back again, up the valley. She saw the yellow eye tilt and take them in, but their presence seemed to invoke no response and the eagle continued, all-seeing and invincible, literally the lord of all it surveyed, past them and on into the wild country at the head of the valley, beyond what she knew were the boundaries of her land.

'You look happy.' His voice brought her back from her daydreaming.

'I am happy. I was watching that eagle and thinking about freedom. That always makes me happy.'

He smiled, waiting for her to continue.

'Release from the imprisonment of the past.' She shook her head, still smiling at the memory. 'I'm thinking about eight years ago, about the time when we finally stopped pretending. Contessina de Bardi died in the October of 1473. She was barely missed and her funeral was a small and private one.' She looked up, feeling the need to explain. 'Lorenzo and I did not consider Contessina's death to be a subject of public concern and we had her buried privately and without any fuss.'

~

VIA LARGA
12th October 1473

'It's probably Clarice who will miss her most.' Lucrezia looks at Lorenzo and, absent-mindedly, he nods and smiles back.

They are walking back, arm-in-arm, the short distance from Contessina's funeral in the Church of San Lorenzo to the Palazzo Medici, as unobtrusively as the Medici can do anything. Along the street people are nodding, expressing their supposed grief, but really just hoping to be recognized, to be able to say, 'I was talking to the Magnificent Lorenzo this morning.'

But Lucrezia can see that Lorenzo's mind is far away. He is nodding to left and right, automatically acknowledging the people, but she knows she might just as well have said, 'Clarice looks good riding a camel,' and his response would have been exactly the same.

Poor Clarice. She and Contessina had always been very similar – pious and domestic in outlook, both committed to *masserizia*, paying attention to the small things of life – saving *piccoli*, and for that reason, both largely ignored by their husbands, who are invariably too busy spending gold florins. Both ignored by Lorenzo in particular, who is already deeply committed to the wider vista, to *magnificentia*, to being and being seen to be a great prince.

She turns and looks at her daughter-in-law. As she turns back, she shakes her head. Poor Piero's dream that in some way Clarice's old-fashioned virtues might tame Lorenzo's greater excesses have proved completely misguided. He has, of course, done what is expected of him, provided her with a good home, a status in society and a baby to look after once a year, and for the rest of the time he has almost forgotten she is there.

She looks at Lorenzo's blank face. He is far away, probably more concerned about his recent purchase of Poggio a Caiano. He calls it his *possessione*, probably because he has been unable to buy it outright and has only gained access to it in instalments. What a circus that has been. Bernardo Rucellai tried hard to prevent his father, Giovanni, from selling the estate to Lorenzo at all, and he has clung on desperately to parts of it for over five years now, after the original purchase agreement had been signed. But bit-by-bit, each a hard-fought clause in the legal agreement, Lorenzo has gained full control of it. Looking back it was probably his having to fight so hard to get it that made him appreciate it so much in the first place. There's not much that Lorenzo has to fight for.

It's a farming estate near Empoli, and amid wonderful rich countryside. She and Lorenzo had quietly surveyed it together years before while the owner was in Venice. They knew from the first it had great potential and Lorenzo had plans to bring in special cattle from Milan long before he managed to buy the place. But first they knew he would have to tame the River Ombrone, and now that's just what he has done. As soon as the purchase was finalized he called in all the experts he could muster: water masters, meadow masters and a canal expert from Viterbo.

She has to admit he'd gone about it in a very professional manner, quite as carefully as she would have done. In overall charge of the works he had chosen Domenico, whom they all referred to as the captain, and between them they set to work on canals, embankments, dykes and channels, which they lined and strengthened with thousands of mulberry and pine trees. By the time they had finished the river flowed safely, even under flood conditions, while the meadowlands, although irrigated, were only allowed to flood in a controlled manner, thus ensuring the annual covering of fresh river silt was not all washed away again.

There's an old house on the estate that once belonged to Rucellai's father-in-law, Palla Strozzi, and it's where she now has a room. She loves it. There's a calm richness to the place that is comforting as she gets older. She can look out of the window and see these fat cattle, as sleek as racehorses, and somehow, when she does, the world seems a better place.

~

Lucrezia leaned back against the rock and closed her eyes. 'Wealth and the freedom to enjoy it. There is no substitute.' To her surprise, the remark was met with an almost deafening silence. She sat up, opening her eyes again and turned towards him. Beside her she saw the monk nod. But somehow he did not look convinced. She stood, thinking, and together they moved on again, climbing more slowly now, avoiding breathlessness and able to talk as they went.

'Although not significant in itself, Contessina's funeral probably signalled the end of an era. It was certainly a time of change. Another big change had taken place some time just before that. The Venetian pope, Paul II, had died and he had been replaced by a della Rovere – Sixtus IV.' She shook her head. 'Sixtus was to become the bane of Lorenzo's life.'

~

PALAZZO MEDICI
October 1473

'It's not all bad.' Giuliano's face does not match his words. But he's doing his best. 'Uncle Giovanni Battista was re-appointed as Depositor General of the Apostolic Chamber, so at least we've secured the Medici Bank as the Vatican bank once again.'

Lucrezia nods. She knows why everyone else in the room is so unhappy. In that new capacity, and at Lorenzo's request, her brother had approached Sixtus to look favourably at making Giuliano here a cardinal.

At the time, Sixtus's response had seemed favourable and they had all felt that it was just a question of time. Indeed, their confidence was increased when Sixtus extended the Medici Bank monopoly over the alum trade, based upon their mines, at Tolfa. It was an agreement that Lorenzo had originally negotiated six years earlier, on the same journey to Rome that been disturbed by Francesco Sforza's death and which had thrown Lorenzo into the depths of a difficult negotiation. That contract extension had been good news. The alum business is still highly profitable and has been a mainstay of the Rome branch for a long time now.

But then, she remembers, they had hit the first of the disappointments. Sixtus had begun appointing cardinals and one after another, they had all been 'nephews'. Pietro Riario came first, in thanks perhaps for his services in handing out the bribes that got Sixtus appointed in the first place. At least he was a good diplomat, although why it was necessary to hand him quite so many clerical appointments and to make him quite so rich, and so soon, had not been clear to anyone.

He was followed by Giuliano della Rovere. He had been the pope's enforcer and one of the greatest soldiers ever to wear the scarlet cap, so once again, there was a degree of understanding when the announcement had been made. But when Raffaele Sansoni Riario came next and was followed by Cristoforo della Rovere and then by Girolamo Basso della Rovere, it was starting to look pretty certain that the Medici weren't going to get anywhere with Giuliano's red cap.

Then, with his cardinals lined up before him, Sixtus had turned his attention to founding a dynasty. With celibacy still the official position in the church, although you didn't need reminding there were many leakages to that ruling, it was time to look to a layman, if only to father the children to carry the name forward to the next generation.

Another nephew, Girolamo Riario, a small-time customs clerk from Liguria, had been chosen for the task. Sixtus' first step had been to buy him a title. Conveniently, the village of Bosco d'Alessandria carried the title *Count* on its tiny shoulders and had been available for only fourteen thousand florins.

The pope then set about finding Count Girolamo a bride. After some abortive negotiations, the count was married to the ten-year-old Caterina Sforza, illegitimate daughter of Galeazzo Maria, Duke of Milan. Then, with the Sforza connection and protection in place, Sixtus had set his eyes on Imola, which sat only fifty miles due north of Florence and was right on the main trade route to northern Europe. Somehow, he had managed to convince Taddeo Manfredi, Lord of Imola, to exchange the town for Castelnuevo di Tortona, thus ceding control of Imola to Milan.

Now Florence found itself threatened, and in order to keep control of his northern border, Lorenzo made a deal with Galeazzo Maria to buy Imola for one hundred thousand ducats. At this Sixtus flew into a rage. He threatened excommunication, which would have rendered all contracts and treaties between Milan and its trading partners null and void; with the rapid prospect of economic collapse. So faced with this threat, Galeazzo Maria had changed his mind and sold Imola to Pietro Riario for just forty thousand ducats.

Relations between Florence and the pope were strained and, to make matters worse, Sixtus had mischievously asked the Medici Bank to lend his family the money for the purchase. Ever-cunning, his intention had been to drive a wedge between Lorenzo and the city and in this he had almost succeeded. But in the end, after much soul-searching, Lorenzo had taken the side of the city and refused the loan to Sixtus.

But now, to cap it all, this morning, further bad news has arrived. Somehow, it seems, Riario has managed to borrow the money from someone else and they say he has completed the purchase of Imola.

And if that is true, then Lorenzo is left high and dry, on unhappy terms with his city, with the pope and with powerful Milan. And with the Treaty of Lodi having collapsed after twenty-five years of peace, Lucrezia is uncomfortably aware just how vulnerable Florence – and Lorenzo – really are.

And that's why they are meeting, to try to sort something out. As soon as Lorenzo arrives. Nothing can be done without Lorenzo. As if his name had just been called, he enters the room. 'What a miserable bunch you all are. Come on. It's not the end of the world.'

'I wish I shared your optimism.' Francesco Sassetti has the longest face of all.

Lorenzo looks round the room and Lucrezia follows his gaze. Even his younger brother, Giuliano, looks miserable. His face is long and very pale. 'What's wrong with you, pastry-face?'

Giuliano shrugs. 'I've got nothing to do. You are run ragged, trying to negotiate new peace agreements, sorting out the bank, keeping the city in order, and I? I have no useful role in life at all. I'm just The Magnificent Lorenzo's baby brother.'

Grins all round. The trouble is, he's right.

Everyone looks at Lorenzo. Perhaps it's because he's the only one in the room smiling and looking confident? Perhaps (more probably) because in the end, it's Lorenzo who makes all the important decisions.

Suddenly, he claps his hands together. 'Right!' Everyone looks up, expectantly. 'This is what we're going to do. I'm going to negotiate a new peace agreement with Venice and Milan and come to a settlement with the pope.'

He looks at Giuliano, who stands, face like a hangdog, shaking his head. 'Good luck in that venture.' In the absence of a rebuke, Giuliano gets bolder. 'And how, when everybody knows Florence is in retreat and the Medici in trouble, are you going to convince our enemies to sit down at the negotiating table and come to an honourable settlement with us?'

Every face in the room reflects Giuliano's doubts. Each one looks miserable. They all look at Lorenzo, who claps hands again, then holds them out, like a magician, producing a magic rabbit from a hat. 'By Magnificentia. How else?' Everyone looks stunned. 'We are going to hold a joust – the greatest joust ever seen in the Piazza Santa Croce.' He turns to Giuliano. 'I am going to call it Giuliano's Joust, in recognition of your twenty-first year, and it will be dedicated to Simonetta Cattaneo, the most beautiful woman in Florence.'

Giuliano's face lights up, as it always does when his lover's name is mentioned. The poor boy is besotted with her. 'Oh, thank you.'

Lorenzo grins. 'Don't thank me. You're going to do all the work. You said you wanted a job. Well, you can organize the whole thing: castles, banners, pennants, brocades, cloth of gold – no expense spared. You will engage the greatest artists, sculptors, architects, artisans, armourers, poets, musicians and cooks, for our delectation. And I, Lorenzo, will foot the bill.'

The room is in uproar. Everyone is happy. Everyone is confident it will be a great success.

Except Francesco Sassetti. 'When is this great event going to take place?'

The room goes quiet. A dampener on their euphoria. The winter is ahead of them. It will be months before the sun returns.

'The end of January!' Lorenzo makes the announcement with a flourish.

'January?' Lucrezia is the only one who dares contradict her son. 'You can't hold a joust in the Piazza Santa Croce in January!'

And Lorenzo, without faltering, turns to her and says 'Can't I? Just watch me!'

Lucrezia looked across at Savonarola and smiled to herself. The monk was sitting on a flat rock, a long blade of grass between his teeth, chin cupped in his hands, obviously lost in her story.

Encouraged by his interested expression, she took a deep breath. 'It's a matter of style, really. *Condottieri* fight with mercenary armies, paid for by the participating parties in a war. They like plenty of show: men, horses, guns, armour, cannons, flags, banners, and noise – always plenty of noise. And the questions they are addressing with all this show? Will this army prevail? Will they break our army? Will they pursue us all the way back to our city walls? Once here, will they besiege us until we are starving and plague-ridden? And if they do, what ransom shall we have to pay to save ourselves from rape and pillage? It all comes down to money. War always does.

'But princes? The questions they face are different. Does he have a clear strategy? Does he have the confidence to carry it out and the persistence to drive it through to fruition? Does he have the confidence of his people? Of his allies? Does he, in other words, have sufficient support?' She raised her eyes, making sure he was still listening. 'And finally, and overpowering in its significance, does he have the money to make it all come true?'

'That is what *magnificentia* is all about: imagery, perception and confidence. Yes, it involves shows, and bands, and flags flying, and armour glinting in the sharp morning air, and banquets loading down tables until they bend, and artists painting heroic pictures, and sculptors hewing rock, and poets reading orations. But above all it's about confidence, theirs in you and, just as important, their perception of yours in yourself.

'It's about advertising yourself, *advertere* – you know your Latin, Girolamo – to make people turn toward you, to make them notice you, and if you can't make them like what they see, at least make them respect it.'

'Lorenzo understood that?'

She could see Savonarola was smiling. And concentrating hard. She could almost hear him remembering, and she knew that he had not only heard her but that despite his resentful upbringing, he understood too.

She nodded. 'He has always understood. Lorenzo was *born* understanding.

'He also left nothing to chance. It was a heaven-sent opportunity. An opportunity to kill two birds with one stone. Giuliano wanted recognition, so Lorenzo announced the joust in his name. Giuliano wanted uplifting, so Lorenzo allowed him to dedicate the joust to Simonetta Cattaneo, the most beautiful woman in Florence, thus associating Giuliano with beauty and success. Giuliano wanted responsibility, so Lorenzo put him in charge of organizing the joust himself. And he did. With the care and precision his elder brother would have taken pride in.

'And in case anybody of influence was unable to attend and see for himself, Lorenzo asked his close friend Angelo Poliziano to write and publish an epic poem *Stanzas Begun for the Joust of the*

Magnificent Giuliano de Medici.'

By his blank stare, it seemed the monk had not enjoyed the benefit of Poliziano's epic work.

'Poliziano described it and just in case the imagery was lost on the less-than-literate, Botticelli repeated the allegory with his paintings of *Primavera* and *Venus and Mars*, with Simonetta seeming to don, or in her case, perhaps I should more accurately say remove, the mantle of the goddess with graceful charm while Giuliano played the male god's role, just to make the point.'

'Was it well attended?' Savonarola's expression looked more well-mannered than really interested, but it was a start.

'They were all there, all Lorenzo's friends – all the beautiful people, as I used to call them.'

~

PIAZZA SANTA CROCE, FLORENCE
29th January 1475

'Ladies over here, men over there. Ginevra, please will you stand with Simonetta and Lucrezia? It's only a bit of fun. Won't take a moment.'

Giuliano has become so accustomed to his organizing role that he can't stop.

'We're lucky with the weather. Lovely light for drawing. Not like January at all.' Leonardo da Vinci, dressed in rose pink as usual, smiles at the girls, obeys Giuliano's instruction and moves along, making room for them. He has been swapping rude rhymes with Lorenzo and his friend Amerigo di Giovanni de Benci, director of the Geneva branch of the bank, who is paying the Florence Tavola and the Palazzo Medici a visit. Amerigo has brought his daughter Ginevra with him and already she is causing quite a stir. She is a gorgeous little thing, just seventeen, and married a year previously to Luigi di Bernardo Niccolini, a tall, thin-faced cloth trader, well-known to be ferociously rich but absolutely charmless.

Bernardo Bembo pushes into the far row between Leonardo and Sandro Botticelli and introduces himself. He has just arrived in Florence as Venetian ambassador and come to the joust with his wife and son, who are somewhere near the back. But Bernardo has heard about the auction and despite his family's presence, he's made his decision already. He's not only going to bid, but when Ginevra comes up for auction, he, and nobody else, is going to be her *Cavaliere Servante*.

It's a piece of fun that Giuliano has dreamed up. He has filled the front row of the crowd with the most beautiful girls and then allowed the men to declare their undying love for them and to be their knight in shining armour. Of course they have to pay for the privilege and in each case the highest bidder wins, with the money going to the poor, less an administration charge, of course, to cover costs, but nobody knows what they are and nobody dares ask the Medici.

Lorenzo is, as always, expected to be the highest payer, but he's seen how the land lies. So when La Bencina comes up for auction first, he bids hard enough to push Bembo to his limit and then gracefully and very publicly retires. This leaves Bembo to claim his prize, which publicly involves a gentlemanly peck on the cheek but privately seems to involve a surprising amount of groping beneath her heavy winter cloak and passing of notes. The girl retires red-faced and breathless to rejoin her father and Bembo, flushed with a combination of success and lust, rejoins his family higher up, in front of one of the wine tents.

Lorenzo opens the bidding again, this time for Lucrezia Donati. This is no great surprise as Lorenzo is known throughout the city for his long-standing relationship (his joke and a very well-worn one) with the fair Lucrezia. Indeed, everyone remembers the rather public snub he delivered to his future wife-to-be, Clarice Orsini six years earlier, when he declared his undying love for Lucrezia at his own joust, and was presented by her with a large bunch of violets. But today, to everyone's surprise, Lorenzo is outbid and for the second time withdraws gracefully.

With Ginevra and Lucrezia 'sold' Lorenzo reappears, this time declaring for Simonetta Cattaneo. He bids steadily, outbidding her husband Marco Vespucci. But then, to everyone's delight, Giuliano outbids his brother and wins the hand of the fair lady, who is promptly declared belle of the tournament. It's hardly news as Simonetta has, by general consent, been dubbed the most beautiful woman in Florence ever since she first arrived from Genoa. No surprise either that Giuliano had to win, as it is no secret that she is his mistress and has been for some months.

The contest ends with loud applause and considerable conversation in the crowd. Down at the front, Leonardo da Vinci is busily sketching Ginevra de Benci. It seems Bernardo Bembo has wasted no time in commissioning a picture of her.

Sandro Botticelli leans over his shoulder. 'You were right, Leonardo. Lorenzo and his brother came to an agreement. This is Giuliano's day and Lorenzo agreed not to spoil it for him.'

Leonardo blows chalk off his sketch and half-turns. 'It's just as well. Giuliano is getting pretty serious about Simonetta. He would have been furious if Lorenzo had outbid him on this day of all days.'

He brushes back his long hair with his fingers, leaving pink chalk marks above his left ear. 'If they'd had a row about it in front of everyone, it would have ruined the day for all of us.'

~

'But they didn't and within an hour we had Botticelli sketching Simonetta on Giuliano's behalf and Leonardo doing the same with young Ginevra for Ambassador Benci.'

Lucrezia had relaxed as her tale unfolded and was now looking more rested than she had for days. She smiled at the memory. 'Every time I looked up there seemed to be an artist handing over a little sketch and some rich man handing his florins in the opposite direction. If Giuliano had thought about it, he could have made it another way of raising money for charity, but the artists were poor enough, so nobody minded that they kept the money.'

'Are they sluts, these women?' To her complete surprise Savonarola's eyes were cold and distasteful.

'Sluts? Of course not. They were respectable married women. And all from good families too.' How can you even think such a thing?

'But they flirt with other men. Pretend to have sexual interest

140

in them. And do so publicly, in front of crowds. What sort of example do they set for others, these so-called women of good families?'

She shook her head, despairing. 'No, you don't understand, Girolamo. It's all a game. Courtly love. As if the men were once again knights in armour, pursuing the art of chivalry and the women are the fair maids they pretend to woo. Everybody does it. It doesn't mean anything.'

'So the men do not, in the end, sleep with the women?'

'Good Lord no.' She paused, thinking of Lorenzo and Lucrezia Donati, of Giuliano and Simonetta, of Benci and Ginevra. 'Well, some of them, perhaps. Very privately and with the utmost discretion. Rich men do … have a tendency to pursue that which they cannot have.'

He looked at her hard and in that look she felt distance, criticism, even perhaps disgust. 'Yes. They do don't they? Until they get it. And then, having ruined it, they don't want it any more.' His face was cold now. 'Do they?'

It is never easy to look into an expression that rejects you and everything you live by so completely, and so she averted her eyes. Looking across the valley, uncertain how to continue, she changed the subject.

'La Bencina, as Poliziano always called her, kept Leonardo busy that year. The ambassador wanted paintings and a marble bust of her. Most of us thought it was because she had refused his approaches and the images were a substitute, but I admit there were scurrilous rumours the other way. Whichever way round it was, his pre-occupation with her continued for a long time.

'Leonardo sold him a painting of her, with juniper trees behind and her eyes looking strangely out of focus, as if she was far away in another world. Leonardo also did the drawings that Verrocchio used to make the marble bust of her, holding a bunch of violets to her breast, a reference to a poem by Braccese, teasing Benci for his broken heart.

'All in all, it was a wonderful day and although it took place at the end of January, the weather was kind to us and we all got home without a soaking. It was the making of my Giuliano – he was taken much more seriously after that, and remained grateful to Lorenzo for what he had done.'

With a dry throat, perhaps after all her talking, and perhaps in response to his look of harsh rejection, she crossed to the stream and drank, then inclined her head. Standards were standards and she was determined to not allow their conversation to become uncivilized.

She smiled, a somewhat forced smile. 'Shall we walk back?'

He nodded his agreement and reached for the walking sticks, left leaning against a rock. As he turned, she felt a sudden pain in her stomach and doubled up. Luckily, by the time he stood and turned back to her she had recovered herself and was smiling again. But the pain this time had been particularly sharp, worse than ever before, and it had frightened her.

Together they set off down the hill, he asking questions about the joust and she answering as best she could. But the pain kept returning and she hoped she could reach the Bagno before he noticed. She had not told anyone – not even her doctor – about these pains and the lumps she had been feeling for weeks. She didn't want to. She knew all too well that once she did, they would confirm it and then, officially, she would be dying. And she was not ready for that, not by a long way.

So until that situation arose, she would hide the pain, smile and live on. It was her life (what was left of it) and she was determined to live it her way.

Chapter 14
Be Warned

He was waiting for her when she got back. Tired and covered with the dust of rapid travel on a fast horse. But as soon as she saw his face she knew he had news for her.

'Benvisto! You look exhausted. When did you leave Florence?'

'Yesterday, at dawn. I rode most of the night, resting only when the horses could do no more.'

'Is someone looking after your horses? Have you ordered food?'

'Both. Please do not worry. Piero Malagonelle saw me arrive. Everything is in hand.'

She nodded, the immediate priorities taken care of. To be effective, as she knew well, good manners involve practicality not just mannerism. 'You have news for me then?' *If he's ridden this hard to bring me urgent news, it's ill-mannered not to seek it immediately.*

'Ser Francesco d'Antonio has good contacts. Efficient ones too. They replied more quickly than I expected.'

She smiled at the name 'He's served me well. An admirable notary. I don't know where I would be without you all.' He looked up, one eyebrow raised. 'My trusted ones. You included, Benvisto. Loyalty with efficiency. It's a powerful combination. I appreciate how hard you have worked to bring me this news so quickly.'

'Loyalty meets its own echo, I believe, Madonna. You are a popular employer. Clear in instruction, fair in judgement, and generous in reward. That's why everyone walks the extra mile for you.'

'Or gallops.' The compliment had delighted her to the point of embarrassment. 'Well then? What news of our monk?'

Benvisto took a document from his leather satchel and opened it. He leaned forward to pass it to her but she shook her head. 'Read it to me. I have mislaid my reading glasses.'

'Girolamo Savonarola. A troubled man, talented but opinionated. A man of high intellect and extensive learning, each exceeded only by his own overly high opinion of himself. Despite his arrogance he was accepted at court in Ferrara and became a member of a noble humanist group, in which he was said to be "highly active".'

Benvisto nodded in emphasis and immediately she realized what her informant meant. Why then the monk's high moral stance? 'But was rejected because of his predilection for inflicting pain on others. The same emerged from Santa Maria degli Angeli. It was said that in the name of religious penance, he almost tortured the young novices to the point that their parents revolted and in the end the bishop, supported by the pope himself, had him relieved of his duties.'

By this time, Lucrezia was staring at her messenger, absorbing every word.

'To save face, they sent him to San Marco, in Florence, in the hope, it was admitted, that the strict observance of the new Dominican order there would either make or break him. Savonarola is said to be a man with a grudge against everyone. He believes himself superior to all others in judgement and adherence to moral codes and seems intent on changing the world.'

Benvisto put the piece of paper down and looked at Lucrezia. 'To use Antonio's very words as I was leaving, a man who is only ever on his own side; a man not to be trusted.'

'Was there mention of a brief love affair?'

Benvisto snorted in derision. 'Oh yes. Brief indeed. She rejected him as soon as he was found guilty of sodomy with three nobles at the Este Court. Apparently it wasn't his first time. His representative had asked for three earlier cases to be taken into account. They say he concocted some tale about her illegitimacy thereafter, but everyone knew she was not a full member of the Strozzi family, not least the girl herself. According to Antonio's sources, by the time he left Ferrara he was a bit of a laughing stock.'

'He told me a quite different story.' Lucrezia was thoughtful.

'As Antonio said, a man not to be trusted. I should say as little as possible to him.'

A servant kicked on the door with his foot, a tray of fresh bread, good cheese, wine and water in his arms. Lucrezia nodded. 'Your supper. I shall leave you to enjoy it. We will talk again tomorrow. In the meantime, my thanks again for your efforts.'

Benvisto gave a small, formal bow and handed her the letter.

As she walked away, her expression was thoughtful.

Chapter 15
Bagno à Morba

He was, as always, punctual. He was, as always, prepared. But today, to his surprise and disappointment, she did not respond to his knock.

He wondered whether his style of questioning toward the end of the previous day had angered her. It had, he acknowledged, been somewhat aggressive, and might easily have caused her upset. Perhaps even upset her to the point of being unwilling to talk? Yet over the last ... *how long is it since our first conversation? Ten days?* They had spoken daily and although some of their conversations had proceeded more easily than others, you could hardly say he'd had to cajole the words out of her. Most of the time quite the opposite. Most of the time, the words had tumbled out of her as if ...

The thought hit him, suddenly and already fully-formed. *Of course. That is why she agreed to talk to me in the first place, and having done so, why she has opened her heart to me so easily. She needed to talk because deep inside, she questions the truths by which she has led her life. That is the voice I have been hearing but not able to identify.*

He nodded to himself and began pacing up and down outside her house. That was it. When she adopted that hectoring tone and started talking down to him like that, she was not patronizing him at all, as he had thought at the time. Not shouting him down to try to convince him. *She was trying to convince herself.*

That must have been why she went so pale just before they set off back down the path yesterday. Her mood had seemed to falter when he began questioning her about the ... what did she pretend it was? Chivalric love? What utter nonsense. Do these people seriously believe that the general populace doesn't see through all that shallow pretence in an instant? A slimy old ambassador slides his disgusting hands over some seventeen year old girl and she is supposed to smile and take it, just because he is rich and he says it's chivalric love?

And the people? The crowd? Does she seriously believe that when a noble professes to a platonic friendship with another man's wife the crowd don't immediately know he is itching to lift her *camicia* and lie between her legs? Who do these people think they are? And how stupid do they think the rest of us are?

Humanism. That's the name they give it when they're being smart and trying to convince the rest of us that they live on a higher plane. Plato's imaginary republic, born again. What rubbish! He had studied humanism at the University of Ferrara and again, later, but with greater cynicism, at Bologna, and he knew exactly what it was. A lie. One great big cynical lie. As if all you had to do to make filth into classical studies was to wear a *guarnacchia*, or a *toga*, or some similar full-length over-gown and pretend you are a Greek scholar.

Look at the paintings they are displaying openly now. One of the last things he had done before leaving Florence was to accept an invitation to see Sandro Botticelli at work on a new painting. *Primavera* he said it was going to be called, *a celebration of springtime renewal and as such, an allegory in recognition of the Medici.* Filth. That's what it was, judging by the preliminary drawings. Young girls in clothes you could see through and all of them with their tits and arses showing. But no doubt, if you say it in a Greek accent and call it *allegorical*, then it seems it's all right. These Florentine people are so cynical.

And the written word is as bad. Humanism they call it, as if everything that is human is somehow to be recognized and respected. But half of what they write is filth. Dante's ascent of the mountain is portrayed nowadays in such terms that the *Mons Veneris* immediately leaps to mind. And by the time Marsilio Ficino has finished with the Orphic *Hymn to the Sun*, metaphors of damp caves leave nothing, yet everything, to the imagination. And they call themselves Greeks!

I read Greek and I write it. Quite good Greek, even if I say so myself. *Pornographos, writing about prostitutes,* that's what it is. And please don't tell me it's just Braccio Martelli and Luigi Pulci who write such filth to each other. Lucrezia stands there and lectures me about her son as if he's a saint. But look at his so-called poetry. Oh yes, make no mistake, I have read it. I have read them all. The *Song of the Bakers* , for example:

Oh pretty women
Such is our art
If you'd like something
To pop in your mouths
Try this for a start

And the *Song of the Village Lasses*:

We also have some bean-pods, long
And tender morsels for a pig,
We have still others of this kind,
But they're well-cooked, quite firm and big,
And each will make a foolish clown
If you first take the tail in hand
Then rub it gently up and down

And then there's that other one, *Song of the Peasants*, that the crowd were chanting together just before I left Florence:

Cucumbers we've got and big ones
Though to look at, bumpy and odd
You might almost think they had spots on
But they open passages blocked
Use both hands to pluck them
Peel the skin from off the top
Mouths wide open and suck them
Soon you won't want to stop

If that isn't filth, I don't know what is.

By this time he had worked himself into a lather of indignation and self-righteousness, but still she had not shown herself, which was perhaps as well. Then Piero Malagonelle appeared, climbing carefully down the steep stone steps that come down the side of her house, a house which, because of the steepness of the ground here beside the river, had had to be cut hard into the cliff-face.

'Are you waiting for Mona Lucrezia?' After what had been going on in his head, Savonarola found Piero's voice calm and soothing.

He nodded. 'We usually talk at this time of day.'

'I know. She sent me to find you. She apologizes, but says she will not be able to meet you today. She has been taken ill, a relapse of some old ailment I understand. We have sent for her doctor who is in Pisa at the moment. But I doubt if he will get here in time.'

Savonarola opened his eyes wide and stared. 'You mean you don't expect her to live?'

Malagonelle began to laugh. 'Quite the contrary. I expect her to recover before the doctor gets here. That's what I meant.' The project manager took his arm. 'I'm going to do my weekly tour of inspection. Would you like to join me?'

Savonarola nodded and fell into step. *This may be an opportunity to ask some inadmissible questions.* He tried the first. 'Does Mona Lucrezia really own this place in her own right, or does it technically belong to her son?'

His companion seemed to have no qualms about replying. 'Oh no. Make no mistake. Mona Lucrezia is a true woman of substance and in her own right. When she married Piero she was already wealthy and had a clause written into the marriage vows to ensure she kept her own assets separate from her dowry.

'Her *paraphernalia*?' His mind was still on the Greek. '*The possessions of a woman distinct from her dowry.*'

His companion tipped his head on one side. 'If you say so. I have no Greek. I content myself with the bible, Latin and books of account.'

They reached the foot of a long row of steps cut steeply into the hillside and one after the other began to climb. Conversation stopped until they reached the top, where the river ran into a huge stone tank, as large as the house below. From it emerged a network of channels and pipes.

'This is the main collecting tank. There's a settling tank higher up, which holds back any silt and means we don't have to clean this large one out every year. We have four more, much smaller collecting tanks, on subsidiary streams higher up the valley, to provide alternative water. Each has a different mix of minerals. The rocks around here are so varied that even short distances can change the chemical composition of a stream completely.

'Some we use for drinking, some for plunge-pools, especially for arthritis, and some for douches. But the main flow – through here – flows on with an overspill forming the little waterfall that refreshes the pool you sat beside with Mona Lucrezia.'

'And she owns all this?'

'She leases the land for fifteen ducats a year. She signed a lease into perpetuity with the Commune of Volterra three years ago, although she had signed a shorter term lease before that when work first commenced. The long lease is conditional upon the continuing flow of three out of the four streams. You can't be too careful nowadays. Ser Francesco d'Antonio, her notary, has been very diligent.'

'And you have improved the accommodation? I assume most of what I saw down below is new?'

'It's all new. And yes she owns all of it outright. In the end we decided to knock everything down and start again. Some of the foundations were weak and we wanted to put a second storey on the top of the guesthouse. The hotel is completely new too – Lucrezia designed it herself, and the same with the wash house. We now have twelve shower rooms as well as the three large pools you have seen and the plunge pools across over there.' He pointed towards the edge of the gorge where the main river fell steeply in a series of waterfalls and cascades.

Slowly, they worked their way downward through the Bagno, examining each pool, building and construction as they went.

'You have to check everything regularly when there's water

involved. We get floods every winter, and some quite heavy spates even in mid-summer. The valley is quite narrow here and there's nowhere else for the water to go. Bridges are washed away, pools fill up with silt and gravel. It's a continuous battle.'

'But a profitable business?' Savonarola was impressed. Whatever reservations he may have had about Lucrezia's family life among the beautiful people of Florence, she certainly knew how to manage a business and motivate her staff. What a difference, he thought, it might have made had she been given responsibility for running the Medici Bank all those years earlier.

The project manager nodded and smiled. 'We can't complain. The *maggese* – the busy period – begins in May and runs right through the summer. We still get visitors during the *settembrina* – from September until the end of October – but then we close for the winter. Then I have my flock to look after in Pomerace.'

'You are a sheep farmer?'

His companion laughed. 'No. Well in a sense, I suppose I am. I am the vicar of Pomerace, and many of my flock do, I admit, act like sheep on occasions.'

'And your customers? They come here in small groups?' The question was unimportant to him, but served to hide his embarrassment.

'In the main. But when the family come, then it's quite different. Madonna Lucrezia usually brings no more than a dozen, so we are relatively quiet, but when the Magnificent Lorenzo comes, poor Giovanni di Pace is run off his feet.'

'He brings a large entourage?'

A small shrug. 'Thirty-three people last time, excluding the soldiers who protected him along the road. Bertoldo di Giovanni, the sculptor, Antonio Squarcialupi, who composes music, two singers, two secretaries, two waiters, a sommelier, five archers, a stable master, two cooks, a wagoner, and assorted grooms and, of course, the servants and hangers-on.'

There was something about the way he said the last phrase that made Savonarola look up. 'What sort of hangers-on?'

'You know.' Emphatically, Piero pursed his lips and shrugged just one shoulder. 'Singers who don't sing. Servants who have no tasks. Pretty boys. And girls,' he corrected himself quickly. 'They're not all boys, by any means. But boys or girls, they're always beautiful. Do you know what I mean?'

Savonarola nodded his head. 'I think so.'

They completed their tour and returned to their starting point. 'I hope you found that interesting.'

'Very. Thank you.' Girolamo Savonarola turned away and began to walk down to his room. There could be no doubt. It was a consistent story and if anything, even worse than he had expected.

Piero waved a hand in farewell. 'I'll tell Mona Lucrezia we spoke. Hopefully she will be better soon.'

Chapter 16
Leonardo's Trial

'We must resume our conversations. I was sorry to let you down yesterday.'

She looked pale, but at the same time the gritty determination he had seen in her face so often before was still there. There was something else too. Watchfulness, almost amounting to distrust that he had not felt previously. He smiled, carefully. It wasn't going to be an easy choice. What he wanted to say to her would, he knew, be uncomfortable and yet he could not, in all conscience, ignore it. Piero Malagonelle must have known what he was talking about.

'Are you sure you want to talk? I sense that some elements of our recent conversations have displeased you.'

He saw her expression change and she shook her head. 'Not at all. I criticize no man for what he believes, nor for speaking his mind. If everyone played the diplomat, we might all go to our graves happy and content, yet universally hated.'

He could not resist a smile. Drawn as her face still was, she was still fiery inside.

'But?' Somehow, he knew there would be a but.

'But I sense you have already come to a number of conclusions, and I fear you may have been premature in drawing them quite so soon. In short, I think you are at risk of being misguided. I have been thinking about our conversation the other day. I know you despise us and consider our lives immoral.' She frowned to herself and shook her head. 'No. Perhaps *amoral* is the more appropriate word for what sits in your head. But in that judgement, I believe you are wrong. That is why I stand before you today. That is why I wanted to talk further as a matter of urgency. Because I did not wish matters to rest where they lay when last we went our separate ways.'

He nodded, accepting what she said, although he no longer thought it applied to her. He had spent an afternoon and evening alone reading. Re-reading to be precise. A book lent to him by Malagonelle, Lucrezia's own *The Life of Tobias*, in *Terza Rima*, in which she clearly excelled. Her use of the form was both skilful and deeply religious. Anyone who read her work soon knew that *amoral* was not a word that should be applied to her. But her son, and his *brigata*? Well, that was a different matter. And perhaps in that juxtaposition lay the problem.

'Do you wish to talk in the house? In the room upstairs?'

She shook her head. 'If it pleases you, I should prefer to walk down by the river, to the place where the flat rock protrudes. The flowing water will sooth my headache and the sound will ...' She looked around her as she said it.

He read her expression in an instant. 'Provide privacy?' Even now he could sense she was uncomfortable speaking in this manner so close to the buildings. The thought rather pleased him, because it suggested that she was intending to tell him some uncomfortable truth, a truth that she had not previously shared with her staff at the bagno.

For the first time that day, she smiled. 'Quite so.'

It was a short walk, down a narrow sandy path with occasional rock steps, herbs and succulents growing on both sides amongst the damp rocks, the sound of the river beckoning them onward. The place she had chosen was sheltered and a dappled light filtered through the trees. Dragonflies hovered around the pools at the riverside and a dipper slid in and out of the water, feeding busily.

'I was re-reading your *Life of Tobias* yesterday. That is not, if I may say so, the work of an amoral woman. Let me make it clear that any moral observations I may make or may already have made do not apply to you, Madonna. It is your son and the *brigata*, his entourage of followers, that I may choose to take issue with.'

She spread the blanket she had brought with her on the rock and sat. 'It is kind of you to make an exception in my case, but I still believe you are wrong.'

She made herself comfortable, perhaps gathering her thoughts at the same time. 'When first we met, you said you wanted to understand how Florence works, what lies beneath the skin of the society you observe and wish to preach to. I would remind you of that request and suggest that you have not only not yet learned how to understand us, but in your relative youth and inexperience, you have jumped too early to too many conclusions, conclusions that are, to my mind, misguided and false.'

He found a suitable rock and sat facing her. His instinct was to argue with her but he resisted the temptation. To do so would prove the very point she was making. He remembered that not only had she been educated in formal rhetoric but had also learned the slippery negotiations of the marketplace. Now was not the time to argue. Now it was better to sit and absorb.

'You are, I think, a strong-willed young man, strongly influenced by the things that happened to you when you were younger, and I suspect that your whole view of the world has become distorted by those experiences. You think you know best and you wish – indeed you plan – to judge others, to be the guardian of their morals and to preach, not only *to* them but, I believe, *down to* them.'

He opened his mouth and closed it again. *Let her speak. I know what I know.*

'But beware you do not fall flat on your face. The Florentines are a worldly lot. Sharp and cynical. They are not great respecters of people, especially of foreigners, and you will have to argue your case well before they give you even a half-fair hearing. And to convince them you will not only need evidence but sufficient knowledge of our society to be able to interpret that evidence correctly.'

Something had changed. Her voice today was not raised. Her tone today was not hectoring. Today she was speaking with the sort of calm, quiet confidence that made even Savonarola listen.

'I am going to give you an example. An example of accusations, of evidence and of the need to interpret that evidence with what I might call local understanding.' He nodded. Listening. 'For the last one hundred years there has been a continuous disagreement between the populace and the educated classes about the battle against crime and, in particular, the fight against the sin of sodomy. The problem is that the common people are too easily swayed by simplistic arguments and sometimes, in their naïve exuberance, they call for harsh laws that, if passed, might easily tear our society apart.

'Quite regularly, the Council of the Popolo have called for a new law, making the act of sodomy punishable by castration, or exile, or death. Yet time and again the Council of the Commune, whilst agreeing with their intentions, have given quite different powers to the *signoria* and the *esecutore*.

'Throughout the city of Florence, we have drums, known as *tamburi*, set beside the roads here and there. They have slots in them, we call them *buchi della verita* – holes of truth – in which citizens are encouraged to make reports to the authorities about any wrongdoing they discover.

'Let me tell you from the beginning that nine out of ten of these accusations are either for tax evasion, adultery, or sodomy; all rightly considered serious offences in a family-based republic. But they are also very easy accusations to make, and exasperatingly difficult to disprove.

'Five years ago, an anonymous accusation was posted in the *tambura* in Vacchereccia, a narrow street leading westward from the corner of the Piazza della Signoria, and opposite the Palazzo Vecchio.'

~

BARGELLO, FLORENCE
Tuesday 9th April 1476

The murmuring in the court stills as the judge rises. 'Read the accusation.'

The clerk now rises in turn and holds up the piece of paper:

To the Officers of the Signoria: I hereby testify that Jacopo Saltarelli, the brother of Giovanni Saltarelli, lives with him at the goldsmith's shop in Vacchereccia, directly opposite the buco. He dresses in black, and is seventeen years old or thereabouts.

This Jacopo pursues many immoral activities and consents to satisfy

those persons who request such sinful things from him. And in this
manner he has performed many things, that is, he has provided such
services to many dozens of persons of whom I have good information
and at the present time, I name some of them. These men have
sodomized the said Jacopo and so I will swear.

They are:
Bartolomeo di Pasquino, goldsmith, living in the Vacchereccia;
Lionardo di Ser Piero da Vinci, living with Andrea del Verrocchio;
Baccino the doublet-maker, living near Orsanmichele, in that street
with the two large wool-shearers' shops leading down to the loggia of
the Cierchi; he has opened a new doublet shop;
Lionardo Tornabuoni, alias "Il Teri", dressed in black.

'There is, as always, no signature.'

The clerk sits and all eyes turn to the five accused, who are standing in the dock looking embarrassed and not a little frightened.

The judge looks at them with a jaundiced eye. 'You are Jacopo Saltarelli, the brother of Giovanni Saltarelli, who lives at the goldsmith's shop in Vacchereccia; Bartolomeo di Pasquino, goldsmith, living in the Vacchereccia; Leonardo di Ser Piero da Vinci, living with Andrea del Verrocchio; Baccino the doublet-maker, living near Orsanmichele; and Lionardo Tornabuoni, also known as Il Teri?'

The five answer to their names.

'You are accused of the crime of sodomy with Jacopo Saltarelli, the brother of Giovanni Saltarelli, and of procuring the said Jacopo Saltarelli for purposes of sexual acts with others, as yet unnamed. How plead you?'

The five reply in ragged unison. 'Not guilty your honour.'

'This court is adjourned until Friday 7th June in order that depositions can be made, witnesses summoned and their statements taken. Until that date you will not leave the city of Florence.'

'The court will rise.'

Shaking their heads the five disperse with their respective friends and relatives. Lionardo Tornabuoni leaves with his

157

lawyer, who has been appointed by his cousin Lucrezia Tornabuoni de' Medici.

Leonardo da Vinci joins his embarrassed father, Ser Piero da Vinci, a well-known notary, who spends most of his working days in and around the law courts, and together they retreat to his office.

Jacopo Saltarelli, together with his brother Giovanni and Bartolomeo di Pasquino, slip down the side of the Badia Fiorentina and cross the Piazza della Signoria as they make their way home to the Vacchereccia.

~

Lucrezia paused to be sure the monk was following her. 'They were brought to trial on Tuesday 9th April. The indictment was read and the case was immediately adjourned, the five accused being ordered to appear before the court in person, on Friday 7th June. On that day, they appeared, confirmed their names, pleaded not guilty, including Saltarelli, and, it being a Friday afternoon, they were remanded again.' Again she looked up. Yes he was still listening.

'Now, you might consider such evidence to be compelling, even if I tell you that one of the Leonardos, the one they call Il Teri was my cousin, while the other one, young Leonardo da Vinci, had been living in the Palazzo Medici for the previous two years and studying sculpture and drawing in the academy, which Lorenzo had established in the gardens there. He was well-known to us and well-liked.' She smiled and wagged her finger. 'But if you did believe such evidence, you could not have been more wrong.'

~

BARGELLO
Tuesday 11th June 1476

This time the court room is full. The Florentine crowd loves a sodomy case. It usually involves one or two nobles and some sad victim from amongst the poor. An opportunity to see the upper classes squirm in embarrassment and sometimes fear.

The penalties seem to vary according to who you are, how

well you have bribed the court officials, and how embarrassing your case is to the Signoria of the time. This is a good one. A Tornabuoni and cousin to a Medici wife. And an artist who almost lives at the Palazzo Medici and who is known to be a friend of Lorenzo himself.

Leonardo da Vinci's appearance in court is not entirely unexpected. He looks every inch a pretty boy. Today he's in his favourite rose pink. Hardly a sensible choice if you are accused of sodomy, but everyone has to admit he looks good standing beside Il Teri in his jet black doublet and hose.

They are well represented. All the top lawyers in town seem to be in this one courtroom today. Lucrezia Tornabuoni's favourite advocate is riffling through his notes one final time and sharing a couple of words with the two lawyers that Ser Piero da Vinci, the well-known notary, has engaged to defend his son.

The indictment is read and the statement posted. Then one of the Officers of the Night and Monasteries makes a little speech about Jacopo Saltarelli.

'According to information received,' he says, 'Jacopo was occasionally engaged as a model for the artists at the *bottega* of Andrea del Verrocchio in the Via de Agnolo, a street in the Parish of San Ambrogio, where Leonardo da Vinci also lived and worked. It was there that the offences are believed to have taken place.'

Glances around the court from the crowd. It's a pretty weak start. Haven't they got eye witnesses, people who happened to be looking through the window while those inside were... In the best cases you get lurid descriptions, bare arses, exposed cocks, all seen 'by accident' by someone 'just passing by'. But today seems a bit tame.

It doesn't improve and the crowd starts to grow restless. The officer supports his accusation by saying the Via de Agnolo and the whole of that part of the *Gonfalon* of Chiavi has a bad reputation with the officers and that Verrocchio, in particular, is believed to have an unnatural relationship with a number of his apprentices. Well, everyone in Florence knows that, but the officer is useless. He gives no evidence and has no witnesses, and the court and the audience soon dismiss his words as self-serving innuendo. As he leaves the witness stand there are hisses and boos from the back of the crowd.

Then they call Saltarelli himself. This is better, the crowd start to whistle. He is a very pretty young boy and dressed remarkably smartly for a mere goldsmith. He admits he is a goldsmith and that he works in that capacity in the Vacchereccia, in the *Gonfalon* Carro. He also admits that from time to time he works as a model for Verrocchio and that Leonardo and the other apprentices there 'had drawn him naked and in many classical poses'.

At this point someone at the back of the crowd shouts 'give us a pose then, bend over' and the judge has to call for silence. It's all getting a bit out of hand.

But now some new names are being dragged into the story, names of people not accused but who cares? The more the merrier. He has also, he admits, posed as a model for Botticelli and for Antonio del Pollaiuolo. This brings knowing winks and grins from the crowd. Everyone knows what Botticelli's like and Pollaiuolo's *Battle of Nude Men* is still talked about in terms that are hardly artistic. But Saltarelli insists that nothing improper has taken place with any of them and without any evidence to support the accusations he is soon dismissed.

Leonardo da Vinci is called next. He looks terrified. From her discreet seat at the back of the courthouse, Lucrezia sighs. *Leonardo! Use your brains.* He has hardly helped his cause. He looks as pretty as Simonetta Vespucci, with carefully-cut shoulder-length blonde hair, a rose-pink tunic, jasper rings on his fingers and soft boots of best Cordoba leather. Lucrezia looks round, gauging the reaction of the crowd. It often influences the judges. She sees one or two people in the audience nudge each other and point. 'He's obviously one of those,' she hears one man say to another. 'How else could he afford such clothes? Sells his arse, like the one in black, no doubt about it.'

She turns to her notary, who is acting as moral support. 'He's wrong. It's another example of people jumping to conclusions. I know where Leonardo had that money from, from selling drawings of Ginevra to Ambassador Bembo.' She sighs again.

'It's all above-board, and obviously so, if only you know the people.'

Once he starts answering questions, Leonardo improves. His voice is quiet but confident, rather refined in this raucous environment and he soon swings the mood of the crowd onto his side. He doesn't try to be clever or play at moral indignation. He simply answers the questions and assures them there is no evidence because there is nothing to have evidence about. It doesn't take long before he too is told to stand down and his case dismissed.

Next Baccino is called, and although he admits he had made the black doublet that Saltarelli is wearing and another black one for Il Teri, who has yet to be called, there is no evidence against him and he is dismissed immediately.

Lionardo Tornabuoni, likewise, has no evidence against him. He has not, he says, had any dealings with Saltarelli personally, although he has, he agrees, bought gold items from the shop where he works, 'as have half the moneyed population of the city.' He too is dismissed within minutes, but not before his own lawyer intervenes to ask him a question.

'Have you,' he says, 'had any dealings with the painter Verrocchio?' Lionardo Tornabuoni says yes he has, that he has bought a number of paintings from him and has recently agreed to give a reference for him in support of a contract. But then, before he can say more, the lawyer thanks him and ends the conversation. It's all very strange and as he leaves the stand, there's a confused murmur from the crowd. What was that all about?

Finally they call Bartolomeo di Pasquino.

'Are you,' they ask, 'a goldsmith, trading in the Vacchereccia?' Yes he agrees. He is.

'And do you have any competitors in the area?' they ask him.

'Yes,' he replies. 'The establishment of Paulo di Giovanni Sogliano is opposite. The *buco* is right outside his door.'

'And who owns that goldsmiths' establishment?'

'It is owned by Antonio del Pollaiuolo,' he replies.

Then they ask him to step down and in his place they call an official of the Palazzo della Signoria.

'Have you had any dealings with Antonio del Pollaiuolo?' they ask him. It seems a strange question, but somehow he seems to expect it.

'Oh yes,' he replies. 'He is bidding for a large painting, for the Palazzo. It has a lot of gold-leaf work involved and he has offered the services of his *bottega* in Vaccchereccia to do the gold-work.' He turns to the judge with a helpful expression. 'In fact it was Paulo di Giovanni Sogliano himself who submitted the contract offer.'

'And who is he competing with for this contract?' It is clear the judge has been well-briefed.

'He is competing with Andrea del Verrocchio,' he replies. 'Verrocchio is using young Leonardo da Vinci as his assistant and Bartolomeo di Pasquino has contracted to do the gold leaf for him. Leonardo Tornabuoni has given them both a good reference and recommended we look at *The Baptism of Christ* in the Church of San Salvi as an example of their work. They completed it less than a year ago and it is outstanding.' He turns to the room. 'Especially the angels.'

The more knowledgeable in the crowd begin nodding. It is accepted as one of Verrocchio's better pieces. Lucrezia sniffs. *Not surprising really. One of the angels was painted by Leonardo and the other was by Botticelli.*

By this time the smirkers in the court room have stopped grinning. They sense that something is amiss. There's something not being said. Then the clerk of the court hands over a piece of paper. 'Do you recognize this writing?' he asks.

'Yes,' says the official. 'It is the same hand that made the contract application, the hand of Paulo di Giovanni Sogliano.'

The clerk of the court says nothing. He just turns the piece of paper round, so could the court can all see it. It is the original accusation.

~

For a moment Lucrezia sat, letting her point sink in. 'So you see, not every apparent sin in the city of Florence is as bad as others would have you believe. There are varying interpretations. So

162

before you call for harsher laws, think about the risks and the dangers. And before you make too many accusations, make sure you check your facts. You could be making a big mistake.'

She stood and gathered up her blanket. Suddenly, for the first time that day, she had a bright smile on her face. 'Shall we go back?'

Savonarola rose and fell into step beside her. They began walking back up the path, climbing the shallow steps to the terrace in front of her guesthouse. She seemed content and said nothing. But in his head was not the conviction she might have hoped.

To him the lesson of her little parable has not been the one she had given, but something quite different. *Be careful who you accuse. The Medici have many friends and the lawyers in Florence, like so many others, are sure to be on their side.*

Chapter 17
The Pazzi Conspiracy

Savonarola took another drink of tepid water and shook his head. He felt muzzy. He had had a bad night. A restless night. A night full of dreams, in each of which he began as the accuser but by the end found himself the accused. He had woken, sweating, knowing he could not leave the issue unresolved, that he must raise the matter with her again. But how?

They disagreed, he and she. That would not have been an insurmountable obstacle if all they had disagreed about was the *interpretation* of the facts, as she seemed to imply. But increasingly he felt he was being manipulated, until by now they found themselves disagreeing about the facts themselves.

In some respects it was understandable. Lorenzo was her son, and not only the fruit of her loins but as *Lorenzo Il Magnifico*, the greatest prince of Florence, the product of her belief, her imagination, her conviction and her persistent influence over many years. Indeed you might have concluded that he was the man she had made him, for his father's influence had, it seems, been wholly negative, almost limited to showing him what not to do. Or to be.

But in her pains to exonerate her son, and to the extent that she could see his imperfections at all, it seemed she had convinced herself that he had been forced into what he was by circumstances, by wars, by politics and by the wants of the people. And that conclusion he simply could not accept. Lorenzo the cork, bobbing helplessly on a wild ocean? Hardly.

For hours he had churned the matter over in his mind, unable to decide how to approach her, but now it was the allotted time. Now he could prevaricate no longer. Now he had to go to her.

Feeling only half-prepared, he climbed the stone steps to her guesthouse and knocked. She appeared immediately, as if she too had been preparing for their meeting. 'Come in. We'll talk upstairs.'

They climbed to the familiarity of the room where their first conversations had taken place. Somehow, the very act of returning made him feel that they had gone full-circle; talked themselves all the way round and back to the place where they started.

While he waited to see if she was going to begin their conversation, as she usually did, his mind returned to the previous day, to the court case and to the indelible perception that the Medici family had used the law and their influence, to create – whether by discovery or fabrication he could not tell – a world in which the apparent misdemeanours were all excusable or, indeed, could simply be denied, because the motive of the apparent accuser was suspect.

But what she did not know was that even before he had left Florence he had had his suspicions. On the night before his departure he had spoken to the Officers of the Night and Monasteries and he had already known the full picture as they saw it, the extent of the accusations and the frequency with which they pointed to the same small group of targets.

'Be honest with me.' The words jumped out of his mouth of their own accord. He had intended only to think them. Her sudden and intense gaze meant he had to continue now. 'It's all pretence, isn't it? The whole image of Lorenzo, Friend of the People?'

To his surprise she nodded, smiling, and then sat demurely. Had she too been thinking overnight?

'Yes. Of course it is. It is now. I told you, early in our conversations, that democracy in its purest sense is unworkable.' Rather than being defensive, as he had expected, her voice had become quiet and reasoning.

'You told your son the same thing.'

'Indeed I did.' Her voice lifted and strengthened. 'But it wasn't me that finally convinced Lorenzo. As I have explained before, as a young man he wanted it both ways. He wanted to be a great prince and he wanted the people to love him for it.'

Wanted it both ways. He heard that phrase and immediately heard its echo from a conversation in the past. Lorenzo, it seemed, had an innate greed. He wanted the sun and the moon, the winter and the summer, to seduce men as well as women and now, in addition, he wants to govern and still to be loved by the people.

Wants? *Wanted* was the word she had used. Did that mean he no longer did?

'You said *wanted*. Does your son not want to be a great prince any longer?'

Slowly, she smiled at his simplicity. 'Oh yes. Make no mistake, Lorenzo is and always will be a great prince. He was born to it.' She shook her head, as if in resignation. 'But he no longer expects or even wants to be loved for it. That's what I meant.'

She lifted her head then rose to her feet and began to pace up and down. Her look now seemed to have changed. Gone was the compliant smile with which she had greeted him. Now her look was hard and defiant.

'Once you have seen your brother slaughtered on the altar steps, it changes everything.' She stopped walking, pointed her finger at him, and glared. 'You don't debate after that. You no longer spend your time consulting, searching for understanding, agreement; a settlement. You don't negotiate.' She shook her head in emphasis. 'Not after that.'

She walked towards him, standing over him as he drew back into the recesses of his chair, her finger now making aggressive stabbing movements towards him. She brought her face within a hand's-width of his own, so close that her eyes were out of focus and he was aware of her breath, as hot and angry as her expression.

'Just remember this. You don't take prisoners when your brother's blood is mingling with your own.'

To his relief she pulled back, walked to the window and stood looking out. When she turned she seemed calmer again, but her eyes were still cold and calculating.

'The year 1478 began with a misconception. We knew we had difficulties outside the borders of the republic. In Imola, as I have told you, we had Riario and Sixtus to thank for that. But at home, as winter turned to spring, we thought everything was going to be all right.

'Life went on. The little ones, Luigia and Contessina, were both born to Clarice and Lorenzo during that year. It seemed that Medici family life could continue as if all was well. Lorenzo sat calmly at home, reading letters and reports, hoping his recently-completed Castello at Volterra would keep the Volterrani and the Sienese quiet and that Milan would be able to keep Riario and Sixtus in their places.

'He was half-aware that there were issues in the Milan and Avignon branches of the bank, but nothing that couldn't wait.' She smiled, still leaning against the window, but it was a cold and cynical smile. 'Life seemed almost idyllic.' She walked across the room and resumed her seat, then looked up at him. 'How wrong we were.' Her smile had become hardened now. 'Just because your eyes are shut and you can't see something, it doesn't mean it isn't there. It's not as if we hadn't had any warning.'

He felt himself frown, more as a message to himself than as a communication to her. A warning? Had he missed something? He saw her note his uncertainty with an almost imperceptible nod and realized that it was intended.

She sat back, knowing she has secured his attention.

'Early in April 1476, the city faced a terrible shock. Simonetta Vespucci, by everyone's agreement the most beautiful girl in the whole of Florence, was taken ill. Lorenzo was living in Pisa at the time, supporting the new University of Pisa which he had re-opened only three years earlier. So concerned was he at the news that he had messengers take him daily reports of her progress.

'Giuliano, still in Florence, was unable to eat or sleep for worry. He was so concerned that he asked Lorenzo to send his personal physician to her aid, which he did. But despite his best endeavours, and to the distress of the whole city, she declined rapidly and on Friday 26 April she died. It was a sign. But to our error, we didn't read it as such. Not, that is, until exactly two years later.'

VIA LARGA, FLORENCE
26th April 1478

It is a Sunday and across the city, the church bells are ringing. Lorenzo, now aged twenty-nine, leaves the Palazzo Medici and begins to make his way down the Via Larga towards the Baptistery and the Cathedral of Santa Maria del Fiore, surrounded, as always, by a group of admiring friends.

As Lorenzo reaches the baptistery, his younger brother Giuliano, who has overslept, after a bad night with his sciatica, hurries into his clothes and begins limping after his brother, accompanied by Francesco de Pazzi and Bernardo Bandini. Although bright, it's a cold day and Giuliano is well-wrapped up. Francesco puts a friendly arm round his shoulder and then lets it slide down his back. Giuliano doesn't realize it but Pazzi is checking that he's not wearing chain mail under his tunic.

Lorenzo has already gone on ahead, accompanied by the seventeen-year-old Cardinal Sansoni and Archbishop Salviati and has taken his expected place, up by the high altar, still surrounded by friends. A couple of priests are beside him, preparing for the service. He looks round for Giuliano and sees him enter the cathedral by the Baptistery door. There's a space next to Lorenzo but Giuliano has left it too late and it will be impossible for him to make his way through the crowd without un-gentlemanly pushing and shoving. It's hardly the Medici way – not in public and certainly not in church – and Lorenzo signals to Giuliano to stay where he is.

The service begins. The voices of the choir lift and fall again to the sung responses. The priests prepare for High Mass and the sacristy bell is rung. The voices in the congregation fall silent and all attention is on the Host as it is elevated before the high altar.

Immediately there's a scuffle near the big door facing the Baptistery. Lorenzo looks up and sees what looks like a fight, close to where Giuliano was standing. What he cannot see and only discovers from witnesses later is that Bernardo Bandini has drawn a sword and thrust it into Giuliano's head. There's blood everywhere as Francesco de Pazzi joins in, stabbing at Giuliano as he falls, stabbing in such a mad frenzy that finally he stabs his own thigh.

Now his blood is mixing with Giuliano's. The marble floor is slippery with blood and men are falling over, some trying to go to Giuliano's aid and the rest – the majority – trying to escape the slashing blades.

As Lorenzo frowns and stretches to see what is happening, both priests beside him draw their own daggers. Lorenzo feels a hand on his shoulder. Half-prepared and by now expecting an attack, he whirls round, hitting the priest in the face with his elbow, but as he does so, the point of the dagger slashes his neck, drawing blood.

But Lorenzo is an accomplished swordsman and already he has his sword in his right hand while his cloak is twisted twice round his left forearm as a shield. The priests drop back as he stabs and cuts then slashes, trying to give himself space. He vaults the altar rail and moves purposefully towards the sacristy door, already with the sound of screams behind him, though whether from Giuliano or someone else he has no idea.

To his left he sees Bernardo Bandini, sword in one hand, dagger in the other, smothered in blood, running diagonally to try to cut him off.

Francesco Nori comes into view, blocking Bandini with his shoulder, but Bandini runs him through with his sword, wrenches it free without stopping, and comes on again. Another arm reaches out to stop him and as Lorenzo reaches the safety of the sacristy doors. His last image is of a dagger slashing – a sleeve, a shirt and an arm torn open.

Then silence.

Heavy breathing. The crash of fists against the heavy doors. But they are closed now and for a moment at least they are safe. Lorenzo, on tip-toe with nervous excitement, scans the faces, ready to kill anyone who so much as looks at him, but they are all friendly faces in the sacristy and slowly they put their weapons down and get their breath back.

'Who was attacked? What has happened to Giuliano?'

It's the first thing Lorenzo thinks of as he puts a hand to his neck and feels blood. Antonio Ridolfi sees his reaction and, thinking the dagger may have been poisoned, grabs Lorenzo's shoulders and begins sucking at his wound and spitting blood all over everybody else in his panic.

'Is Giuliano safe?' It's Lorenzo's only concern, more so when nobody will make eye-contact with him or answer his questions.

Things are beginning to look bad. One of his friends, Sigmondo della Stufa, clambers up to the choir loft and looks over the frieze into the body of the cathedral below. The tidal wave of panicking people seems to have turned into a mob, but it's a mob departing. Everyone, Sigmondo says, is streaming out of the doors at the far end and shouting like baying hounds for the killers. 'This is no time to be a running priest with a dagger in your hand,' he says.

They unlock the side door and look out. All is quiet. Everyone is at the other end of the cathedral. They bundle Lorenzo out and the group slips quietly up the lane, behind San Michele, between the Pucci houses and back round through the narrow alleyways beyond to the Palazzo Medici. They reach home and close the doors. Time to get their breath back. Time to think.

Across the city, at the Palazzo della Signoria, archbishop Salviati enters, accompanied by Jacopo Bracciolini and a group of other men. They announce that they have an important message for *Gonfaloniere* Cesare Petrucci, from Pope Sixtus IV. The messenger interrupts the *Gonfaloniere* and the priors of the *Signoria* at their midday meal.

'Take the archbishop to the reception hall,' Petrucci responds. 'The rest can wait down below. Put them in the chancellery if the numbers get too large.'

He finishes his meal and joins Archbishop Salviati who, to his surprise and growing suspicion, is shaking like a leaf. The archbishop begins to deliver his message, but keeps looking at the door and forgetting his lines. As Petrucci's suspicions increase, he calls for the guards, at which point the archbishop breaks for the door, yelling to his companions to 'call the Perugian mercenaries'.

170

But they haven't done their homework. The chancellery has special doors, locked only from the outside and the mercenaries are trapped within. Petrucci goes into the corridor, pursuing the archbishop and is leapt upon by Bracciolini who, hesitantly, draws his weapon. But the *Gonfaloniere* is too much for him. He grabs Bracciolini's hair and throws him to the ground. Then, his anger up, he grabs a metal cooking spit and attacks the archbishop and his men, scattering them.

By the sound of splintering wood, the Perugians seem to be escaping from the chancellery, so the *Gonfaloniere* and the priors run to the tower, lock the doors and climb to the top, where they start ringing the *Vacca*. As the great bell tolls, crowds form in the Piazza della Signoria.

From one corner of the Piazza Jacopo de Pazzi appears, leading a group of armed men on horseback and shouting *Popolo e Libertà*. They ride round, trying to egg on the crowd, but when the priors appear at the top of the tower, hurling rocks onto Pazzi and his men, the crowd turn against them.

From the north side of the Piazza, another group emerges, armed and mounted Medici supporters. They ride up to the Palazzo della Signoria, sheath their weapons and enter. In no time they find the Perugians and with pikes and swords they slaughter the lot. They reappear, with the Perugians' heads on their pikes and seeing this, Pazzi and his men gallop away to the east.

Somehow word spreads that the Pazzi family are leading a revolt and the mood of the crowd grows angry. They begin roaming the streets, attacking Pazzi people and properties. Others race to the Palazzo Medici to give support. They call for Lorenzo, who appears, bloodstained and with a bandaged neck on the balcony. He addresses the crowd. 'The Pazzi have led a conspiracy,' he tells them. 'My brother Giuliano has been brutally murdered, but as you see, I am only lightly wounded. Keep calm. All is now under control.'

But 'keep calm' is the last thing the crowd want to do. They want blood. They rush to the Palazzo Pitti and find Francesco de Pazzi lying in bed with his stabbed thigh still bleeding. They haul him from his bed, drag him to the Palazzo della Signoria and up to the *Gonfaloniere's* quarters. Petrucci wastes no time. He finds Pazzi guilty, has him stripped naked and with blood still pouring from his thigh, ties a rope round his neck and flings him out of the window. As the rope jerks tight, the crowd cheers and jeers and yells for more.

Now they find Archbishop Salviati and drag him in. They strap his arms behind his back, tie a rope round his neck and, still in his archbishop's robes, hang him from the window bars. Kicking and screaming, desperately trying to save himself, he bites Pazzi's body, and hangs on to it with his teeth, as again, the crowd howl with delight.

~

'What a situation!' Savonarola felt the need to show his appreciation, although quite where she thought all this was leading was not clear. Her story had been unfolding so fast he could hardly keep up.

'That wasn't the end of it.' Lucrezia's voice sounded triumphant. 'The people searched everywhere. They found the two priests three days later, hiding amongst the Benedictine monks in the Badia Fiorentino. No trial was required and none held. The crowd tore off their robes, castrated them and hanged them on the spot.'

'Justice or revenge?' Suddenly Savonarola found himself revolted, not so much by the story itself as by the pleasure she seemed to be taking from its telling.

With a wistful expression on her face, she shook her head. 'When the blood-lust of the crowd shows itself, the one becomes the other.'

'Didn't any escape?'

Again she shook her head, this time more emphatically. 'Only Bandini. The rest were accounted – for. Years before, with Pitti and the Party of the Hill, Piero had been lenient. But almost to a man, they had come back to haunt him. Lorenzo had learned from that. This time, apart from Bandini, he made sure there were no survivors to keep him awake at night.'

She looked out of the window counting, remembering, and, it

172

appears, calculating. She had been speaking so fast that there was a dribble of spittle down the side of her mouth. Absent-mindedly, she wiped it away with the back of her hand, her mind elsewhere.

Then she turned. 'You cannot afford to forget too quickly, nor can you allow the people to do so either. Lorenzo talked to the *Signoria*. "Paint them," he said. "All eight of them, including the escaped Bandini, who will be hunted down ruthlessly. Paint their images, life-sized. Let the world know that my arm is long. Tell the world that wherever he goes, Bandini will not avoid me. I shall find him and when I do, I shall have him brought back here in chains. And then I shall have him hanged."'

'Did they do as he asked them?' Savonarola was caught up in the urgency of the story himself now.

'They did as he ordered.' She turned her head sideways and gave him a twisted grin. 'It was not a request.'

She looked out of the window again and then turned back. 'Sandro Botticelli did the *fresco* on the side wall of the Palazzo della Signoria. Lorenzo paid him the forty florins himself, from his own pocket. It took Sandro twelve weeks, working high on a scaffold. All eight of them, he painted. Life-sized, full-length, their faces recognizable, their clothing as they wore in the street, lest anybody mistake them. Bandini alone was painted upside-down, hanging by his ankle. Underneath his body Botticelli painted an inscription, which had been written by Lorenzo himself.'

A fugitive who has not escaped the fates
For on his return, a far crueller death awaits.

Savonarola felt her looking at him and thought her expression was merciless. For a moment, he felt fear. Many times he had heard stories about the fury of female animals, protecting their young. Now, to his consternation, he was seeing it for himself.

'Nobody murders my children, especially in church. I won't have it.'

She lifted her head and seemed surprised that her story had

reached its ending. As her breath returned, her mood seemed to subside. 'The pope wasn't pleased when they told him his archbishop had been hanged and painted in his robes. A few months later we signed a peace agreement with him and King Ferrante of Naples. He made it a condition of the settlement that Archbishop Salviati's image must be painted out. Lorenzo agreed.'

Savonarola looked up, surprised.

The smile on her face had become a smirk. 'Yes. He agreed. But then he took the pope at his word. They over-painted the archbishop's image in white, so it stood out from the others. But they left his name and the inscription underneath.'

Again she looked out of the window. He could see her mood was becoming brittle and melancholy. But as she turned back he could see it was still fiercely strong and unwavering. 'It took two years to find Bandini. He had escaped to the coast and travelled as far as Constantinople in a Venetian galley. But Lorenzo's supporters found him, and the Turkish Sultan honoured his extradition request, sending him back in chains.' She nodded, vindicated.

'They hanged him, still in his rusty chains, with his wife beside him, for good measure. A promise is a promise and Lorenzo had promised Giuliano's body that he would do so. And as for his wife; she should never have aided and abetted his escape. It was a slow hanging. They didn't drop him onto the end of the rope so his neck broke instantly, as they normally do, and as they did for her. No. They hauled him up from the ground, slowly. Using a thick rope. He was strangled, choked slowly and painfully, his eyes bulging in agony.'

'You were there? You saw it?'

'I watched. I can't say I enjoyed it, but I was glad I was there. For Giuliano. For my son.'

'The memory has stayed with you? An image burned into your mind?'

She nodded, and for the first time he could see tears in her eyes as she remembered. 'Yes I was there. Young Leonardo da Vinci was there too, not far from me in the crowd. I watched him, looking and sketching, and afterwards, I saw the page in his little book. As usual he was precise, the pen drawing not large but a good image, and beneath it notes in his magic mirror-writing that only he could read. I asked him what the words said and he read them for me. "Small tan-coloured berretta; doublet of black serge; a black jerkin, lined; a blue coat, lined with throats of foxes and the collar of the jerkin covered with stippled velvet, red and black. Black hose, Bernardo di Bandino Baroncelli."

'When it was all over, Lorenzo wanted Bandini's figure re-painted to show that we had found him and done as we promised. Botticelli couldn't do it, he was in Rome doing some work in the Sistine chapel for the pope. So Lorenzo asked Leonardo to do it. And he did. People said it was the only painting they both worked on. But that wasn't quite true. They had both worked on *The Baptism of Christ*, with Verrocchio. But this was the only fresco they ever shared.

Quickly she waved a finger, to correct herself. 'Except it wasn't really. Because Leonardo used the same trick as he had done on the Verrocchio. While Botticelli had painted the original fresco in *buon fresco*, using *tempera* paints into the still-damp plaster, Leonardo was re-covering an over-painting. He could, of course, have chipped off all the old plaster and started again with fresh *intonaco*, but instead he left the old paint in place and used oil paints to paint *a secco* over the top. Of course, with new oil paint applied on a white under-painting background, Bandini's image shone out against the other figures.' The smirk again. 'As it was meant to.'

Slowly her expression softened from smirk to smile, a mother's smile, reserved for children. 'Botticelli didn't mind. He and Lorenzo were ...' her expression tightened as some further thought seemed to enter her mind. 'But I don't expect you want to know about that.'

As if waking from a dream, she suddenly turned and walked across to her chair. Her movements had become brisk and business-like, as if her memories were being put away in a cupboard and the door closed and locked.

She sat and composed herself. 'Well that's the end of my little story. I hope its intention is clear. The point is, the Lorenzo you see now is the Lorenzo shaped by that experience. It isn't easy to see your brother die. Not like that. You find yourself somewhat short of … sympathy. It makes you resilient and unforgiving.'

She stood up from the chair again and walked towards him, leaning over for emphasis. 'But it doesn't make you a bad person. Not in my book.'

She straightened, turned, walked to the window and stood, looking out, her back to him.

Realizing that he had been dismissed, he got up and without a word left the room. As he descended the stone steps below her house he paused and looked back. *There won't be many more of these conversations now. She's nearly finished.*

Chapter 18
Final Confession

For the next three days she did not speak to him. She couldn't. But at the same time, she felt trapped. Part of her felt she had said enough – all she had to say – and yet somehow she could not bring herself to walk away either, because she knew that once she did, it would all be over and she would never be able to start again.

It's like death she thought. *It's so horribly final. However well-prepared you think you are for it, when it comes to the event, it's still a very big step to take.*

She was prepared for death. Well, almost prepared. She had said her goodbyes to most of those that had mattered. To Giovanni, the only one, apart from Lorenzo, who really mattered.

And to Cosimo. *At least he apologized in the end. I never forgave him for stealing my life, for that is what he did. He sacrificed me for the sake of the family.* She felt her jaw ache and realized she was grinding her teeth together. *But in the end, he paid the price – my price. I kept my son but Cosimo lost his bank. It is mortally crippled now. Serves him right.*

And then there was Giuliano. She had said her goodbyes to him, although he, poor soul, had not been present at the time. But she had been sure he was watching, perhaps with his one remaining eye. She shuddered at the thought. They said the dagger had gone through his eye. Was he still walking round like that? Perhaps all wounds were healed once you got to heaven? Had that been true for Saint Catherine and Saint Sebastian and the other blessed martyrs? She hoped so.

And she had said goodbye to Maddalena. Always she had thought a kindred spirit, although they had been so different in so many respects.

She folded her clothes and absent-mindedly began putting them into one of her travelling chests. They would be leaving soon.

Maddalena's face came back into her mind. *Perhaps, on reflection, not entirely a kindred spirit. There was never any malice in Maddalena. Judging by her journal, she had forgiven Cosimo everything. Perhaps she was right. Each of us to her own. We find our own solace in our own way. In the end, you have to be true to yourself. Make your decisions and stand by them.*

She folded another *camicia* and put it on top of the others. Dear Maddalena. Their final conversation had been a strange one. She had stood alone in the chapel of the Convento di Santo Damiano looking at that crushed pew and the great hole in the roof above it, and Maddalena, she sensed, had been somewhere nearby, invisible, yet watching and listening. And she had spoken to her, silently, and she was sure she had heard her reply.

Now only Lorenzo was left, and saying goodbye to him would have to wait until the very end. Judging by past conversations, it would not be an easy one.

~

PALAZZO MEDICI
May 1472

So, Lorenzo? The work is done?

Lorenzo is standing at a table, his head down in a book. He nods but does not turn or look up. What she can see of his face seems less exuberant than she might have expected, which lends credence to her worries. She ploughs on. 'The tomb has been sealed and consecrated?'

He nods again, head still down. 'As we agreed. It looks good. Andrea del Verrocchio has done well. A fine piece of work.'

Lucrezia swallows hard. He's not making it easy for her. 'And little Cosimino has been reburied in San Lorenzo alongside Giovanni and Piero?'

'Beneath them, to be precise. Apparently there are rules.' Still no eye-contact.

'And the gold?'

Lorenzo's face begins to lighten. 'Downstairs. In the vaults.' Then, with a flourish, like a magician completing a trick, he stands, turns toward her, and laughs. 'It was just as the poem

178

had said. One hundred and eighty thousand shiny new florins, all in leather bags, stacked all round the base of the tomb, in the centre of the courtyard. We had taken a coffin in which to remove the body – luckily a very large one, far too big for a six-year-old boy, so there was plenty of room to stack the bags around it. Then we re-sealed the tomb, closed the coffin and off we set, back here. It was that easy.

'We unloaded the gold when we got here and the next day had the coffin, with Cosimino's little coffin inside it, taken over to San Lorenzo, where he was placed reverently into the new tomb.'

'Who helped you?'

He pulls a face, shrugs. 'A couple of servants.'

As he replies he looks away again and she knows the morning's rumours have some foundation. The household is buzzing with a story of two recently-arrived Medici servants who quickly disappeared again and have just been found, garrotted on the banks of the Arno.

She decides to approach him slowly. Her moment will come. 'What are you going to do with it?'

'With what?' He's being careful now, and obtuse, his head back in the book. It's his way when he feels vulnerable.

'With the gold. The gold you brought from the tomb. What are you going to do with it?'

'How do you mean?' He's being silly now.

'Well, it seems to me you have two basic choices, and I was wondering which of them you planned to pursue.'

He tips his head on one side and pulls a confused face. He can be infuriating when he's like this, but she knows how to remain calm and chip away at him.

'Either you pay it into the bank and make it solvent again. All you have to do is put it through the books as a repayment from the Milan branch of the money owed by the duke.

Still bending over the book, Lorenzo half-turns and sticks his lower lip out. It seems he's not impressed with that plan.

'Or you can take the money as your own and spend it on *magnificentia*; on becoming a great prince.'

'I already am a great prince.'

'An even greater one, then. You know what I mean.'

He nods, straightens, turns, but his face has clouded with suspicion. 'What do you think I should do, Mother?'

She sees no point in prevarication. 'I don't think you need the bank. Not in the sense that we relied on it to build our political position in the past. So long as it makes a steady profit and pays reasonable dividends, we don't need the great surpluses we once did. So if I were you I would let the bank fend for itself and I would invest in my greater reputation.'

Lorenzo nods. 'My greater reputation. Yes.'

For a moment Lucrezia considers returning to the two dead servants. But she can't just crash into it, she needs an introduction. She walks to the window, looks out, trying to look relaxed, and tries changing the subject completely.

'I was thinking about Maddalena earlier today. What did you think of Maddalena?'

She sees Lorenzo's head go back in surprise, but immediately he recovers and pulls a quizzical face. He's thinking, calculating, inventing, off on another perhaps false, trail.

'Olive oil.'

'What?' Now she's the one on the back foot.

'She was the olive oil of our household. The necessary lubricant. The essential ingredient.' Lorenzo's eyes are crafty, but confident. Her confusion must be showing. 'When you prepare simples, of green leaves, you make a dressing, do you not?' She nods, confused. 'So. Contessina was the lemon juice; she always brought a tart sourness to the occasion. Cosimo was the garlic; basic, earthy yet essential. And Maddalena was the olive oil that bound it all together.'

'Oh.' She feels an unexpected pang of jealousy.

'What's the matter now?' His eyes have softened slightly, but he's still standing by the table.

'Is there no place for your mother in this dressing?' As soon as she has spoken she regrets her words. Lorenzo hates people fishing for compliments.

This time he smarms over and hugs her. 'Don't be silly. Of course! You were always the *balsamico*, one tiny drop of which

180

transformed the whole flavour, and which eased our troubles and healed our wounds.'

Now she knows he is being unctuous and they both know she deserves it. Never try to cajole a compliment out of Lorenzo. He will either refuse or else smother you in honey-tongued flattery until you are embarrassed by the excess. Apart from Contessina, of course, who has always accepted such exaggerated treatment as her due and basked in it.

She decides to return to Maddalena. 'So she was perfect, then? Perhaps you are right. She was more than a friend to me, in my childhood and … in my marriage.' She shakes her head at a memory. 'She never really forgave Cosimo, you know.'

He shakes his head. She knows he doesn't need to ask what about. 'No she didn't, did she? She was the only one to stand up to him and to tell him what she thought, wasn't she? In no uncertain terms I believe?'

She smiles at her son's clear reminiscence of an event that took place long before he was born. 'The only reservation I might have is that she was simplistic in her faith.'

'In Cosimo or in God?'

'In God. She may have come to see Cosimo's weaknesses in his later years, and in all honesty there were enough of them, but she trusted God explicitly and absolutely.'

'And you don't? Don't tell me your sacred poems are all insincere? Not after all these years?'

Lucrezia shakes her head. 'Of course not. But there was a huge difference between our respective interpretations of our faith. Maddalena truly believed that God controls every aspect of our lives, that somehow he makes every tiny decision himself and all we can do to influence things is to offer him our prayers.'

Lorenzo sneers. 'Or pay some fat priest to do so on our behalf. If you believe what they tell us, their prayers count much more than our own humble mutterings.'

Lucrezia waves his rudeness away. 'Don't be blasphemous. It's inappropriate and it doesn't help. Holy men have their place, Lorenzo, in your world as well as mine.'

Lorenzo wrinkles his nose dismissively. She understands. His trust in priests has been severely stretched since Giuliano was murdered in the *duomo* itself. But his original question has hurt her and she wants to answer it. If only for herself.

'I believe in God. Absolutely and explicitly. But I have spent my life running businesses as well as trying to keep this family together. And what I have learned is that you can't watch every tiny event unfold and you can't make every single decision yourself. It's impossible. After many years of thought, I have come to the conclusion that God places us in this world, each with certain abilities, attributes and, yes, weaknesses. After that, he tries to guide us, but the decisions in life are ours to make and the responsibility for the outcomes of those decisions ours too. Not God's.'

Lorenzo is watching her thoughtfully. 'And the priests?'

'They are here to guide us. And to help us talk to God and interpret his responses.'

'Like ambassadors?'

'Perhaps. Something like that.'

'Some of them with ambitions and purposes of their own?'

She nods, remembering how many ambassadors Lorenzo has dealt with in his life already. 'Of course. Everyone has. It's a logical consequence of God giving us options and choices.'

Lorenzo is grinning now and she knows that at least for the moment he's on her side. Now is as good a time as any to ask him the question. 'So what happened to the two servants?'

Immediately, Lorenzo's brow is hooded again, and his expression guarded. 'What two servants?'

She keeps her voice light, conversational. 'The two servants who helped you lift the gold out of Cosimino's tomb. The two who helped you fill the coffin. And empty it again later before Cosimino was re-buried in San Lorenzo.'

There's a long pause. She knows her son is thinking hard. 'They died.'

'Died?'

'Haven't you heard? They were found dead this morning. On a mud bank beside the Arno. Opposite the Palazzo Bardi.'

'What happened to them?'

Lorenzo shrugs. 'No one quite knows. From what I heard, it seems they were garrotted.'

'Who by?'

He shrugs again, dismissively. 'I haven't found out. I had paid them handsomely. Perhaps they waved their money about too freely.'

She looks at him long and hard. She knows he's lying. And she knows she'll never discover the truth. And nor, if they have any sense, will anyone else. She sighs. 'Oh dear. What an unhappy ending.'

Lorenzo looks wistful and she knows he's acting. 'At least the secret's safe now.' He gathers up his sword, his dagger, his books and his outdoor clothes, and leans over her. 'Must go, mother. Lots to do. Bye.'

~

Lucrezia shook her head. She had never dared approach the subject again. It was obviously impossible. Playing the part of Lorenzo's mother had been a lifetime role, a task without end. On some days it had been like participating in a serious fencing contest. You could not just cross your fingers behind your back, say enough, and then drop your guard and turn and walk away. But difficult and sometimes uncomfortable as it had been, she would not have missed a moment of it. In the end, being Lorenzo's mother had made up for all the other disappointments in her life – even the big one.

Now she knew the bulk of her life was in the past. Little awaited her in the future except death. Somehow she didn't think it would be long now. Perhaps as little as one year. She hoped it would not be too painful when it came. But also not so quick that she was caught out... unfinished, unprepared. She would never forgive herself if she died with loose ends untied. She did have standards to maintain after all. And a reputation. Of sorts.

After a few days of prevarication, with much packing and unpacking of clothes, she finally made her decision. *I will talk to the monk once more, at the end of the week. On Sunday.* Somehow, she thought, a Sunday would be appropriate. Then he really should return to Florence and face the music. She had kept him long enough. And anyway, by then there would be no more to say.

Apart from the confession itself. She laughed inwardly. *Only the hard part. And then it will all be over.*

Sunday morning came and an enormous thunderstorm was raging. The rain was hammering down on roof tiles and yard-stones alike, raising splashes knee-high. Gutters were overflowing and the river was howling. A veritable torrent of thunderous, uncontrollable dark-coloured water. The sky was black, so dark they had had to light all the lamps and candles and now they had to close the shutters to prevent the violent little squalls from blowing them all out again.

They met for the last time, in the same room, as arranged.

'Thank you for waiting. As I told you the day before yesterday, this will be our last conversation; my final confession. Tomorrow, it will be time for you to return to Florence and I ... I shall go on to Pisa. And after that ...' *Who knows after that?*

She pointed him to his chair, but for herself she chose to stand. She had thought about it for hours and this was what she had decided. To be in a chair was to be a prisoner, and for someone already feeling constricted by her thoughts, that would have been uncomfortable.

No. Today she wanted *him* to be seated, held down, a passive receiver, while she had the opportunity to pace, to look out of the window for the inspiration she had so often gained there and to walk the stage. For this, being her true confession, it must be delivered faultlessly.

She had chosen not only to be on her feet, with freedom of movement to assist expression, but also to be dressed in a high-necked *cioppa* of *pavonazzo*, a careful choice, the dress brought with her in case of special occasions, such as funerals. It was dark blue, almost the iridescent colour of a peacock's back, a sign, not specifically of mourning but more of occasion and by the knowledgeable, always recognized as such.

So here she was, standing, facing him, looking down on him as he sat captive in his chair in the corner, exactly where she wanted him.

'Where do I start? I have told you something of my life, of the events that have happened to me and affected me and those which I, sometimes, have managed to influence myself. I hope in the process I have given you some insights into Florence, the city, its ways and the difference between some of its pretences and its realities. Now, as I reach the end of my story, I must look at my own life with a true and honest eye and confess my sins.'

Well, some of them. Perhaps not all.

She turned away and walked toward the window, already looking out for inspiration, for guidance. Already her mind was repeating the processes of recent days, thinking, filtering, redacting, editing the thoughts cramming into her head into what she should tell him and what she should avoid.

Her difficulty, the main reason she had delayed talking to him until now, was that her conversations with him, although designed to convince him of her truths, had so often, either through his words or by his simple reactions to hers had the opposite effect. Progressively in recent weeks his responses had influenced her, changed her, so that what she would have believed and said a month ago had shifted and now she found herself unsure exactly what she did believe.

The monk, she was not afraid to admit, at least to herself, had done well. He had listened to her. Listened carefully. And in the main, he had said little. But what little he had said – and more importantly, what she had read on his face – had shown how much he despised the way of life she had been describing.

She had also learned how cynical he was about the morality of the stances she had taken and the actions she had, for years past, accepted as normal and, on occasion, had actively tried to defend. And with her morality questioned by so perceptive an audience, she had begun to question it herself.

And there lay the problem, the great unanswered question. If this young confessor had rejected her morality and found it wanting, what would Saint Peter do when the great day came and she was standing on the steps? That final day, when it was too late to change anything?

At the core of the uncertainty was not the conduct of her own life, which, by-and-large, she still believed to have been an honest one, but her legacy. She had spent half her life confident that she had given birth to a great prince, one who would be remembered for generations. But now she found herself beginning to wonder whether, although pursuing her best endeavours with sincerity at the time, she had, in reality, nurtured something of a monster.

Lorenzo. Always an enigma; even in his youth. She returned to his friendships. Her son had always been surrounded by his *brigata*, the golden people, humanists, poets, sculptors, architects, painters, writers. But if she thought about them, remembered them, flooding precociously through her house and gardens, she had to admit that what she remembered most clearly was not people of intellect and creativity, as he had always liked to describe them. No, the most consistent common feature she remembered was their youth and their physical beauty. And not just Lucrezia Donati and Simonetta Vespucci, but the other girls, the low-born girls, those who had come and gone, usually under-dressed but always beautiful. Somehow they had never seemed to last very long.

And then there had been the boys. Some (very few in truth) had been like Leonardo da Vinci, who would cause your mouth to open in amazement at his creative ability, but who was, at the same time, decorative, slender and beautiful in his own right. She could hear his lute playing now, and watch him throw his long hair back as he caressed the strings. And his drawings ... well.

Sandro too could leave you breathless with his work, although as a person she had always had her reservations. Privately that calculating, louche smile had always made her feel uncomfortable, and despite Lorenzo's carefully-worded denial, her memory of late had kept returning to the knowing looks the two of them had so frequently exchanged, and she found herself hoping that the secret they reflected was not the one she feared; the one whose image she occasionally had to repulse from her consciousness.

And then there were the rest, like Alessandro the lute player and Jacopo Saltarelli, that boy who had appeared in the court case. She knew they weren't truly talented artists. And what about that sulky little boy with the golden curls they said was a model at Verrocchio's studio? The one Sandro Botticelli used to snigger about to Lorenzo and say he was addicted to zucchini and cucumbers?

She had ignored them, of course. Lorenzo in that sniggering mood had always been best avoided. But deep-down she had known what they meant. She wasn't stupid. She had just been … how had Lorenzo described her once? *Partially-sighted*. And of course, knowing Lorenzo, he had meant it as a compliment.

All those pretty boys. What had they meant to Lorenzo? Almost certainly nothing. They had just been food. Something to be consumed. Food for the sort of appetites that weren't discussed in polite company. But so what? The rich had always fed well and, no doubt, they always would.

But did that make it right? Perhaps it was time to see with both eyes now? The more she thought about it, the more she found it hard to believe that St Peter saw the world as Lorenzo saw it, even if her son did go to Mass every day.

She thought it was Luigi Pulci who had once said: "Lorenzo, glamorous, charming, brilliant and above all, powerful, Lorenzo was never the seeker but always the sought." Was that, as she was sure her son would argue, simply the way the world was? She knew that with the possible exception of Lucrezia Donati none of them had really meant anything to Lorenzo. She could hear his voice now, a mixture of disbelief and ridicule. "Come on, Mother! If I am hungry and I see bread, I eat it. Are you suggesting I should consider the bread's point of view before doing so?"

No, Lorenzo would never understand.

And now, since talking to Savonarola, a new question had entered her mind. Something she had never considered in all those years. What did those passing relationships mean to the others? To the young girls, proud to be deflowered by a loving noble prince? To the hungry wives, dissatisfied with their husbands and seeking true love elsewhere? And the pretty boys? What of them? Did they, perhaps, believe that their love for the great one had been (at least in their case) reciprocated, even for a moment? Or was the half-florin in their hot little hand the beginning and end of the matter?

Of course, Savonarola was biased in his view of these things by the experiences of his own youth, but even so. He had made her think and she wasn't sure she liked the direction her thoughts were now taking.

She didn't pretend to know the answers, of course. But now, at least, she was aware that the questions existed. At least in the minds of some others. And if they were basing their judgements on the monk's perspectives, what other aspects of the life she had led Lorenzo into would they seek to examine?

The real question, she now thought, having spoken to the young monk at some length about it one evening, was whether people with real power had any responsibility for the imbalanced relationships that formed around them? Did the powerful prince, as a consequence of his wealth, have any special responsibilities toward the pregnant servant girl he discarded? Cosimo had shown the way with Maddalena and Carlo. But then he had loved her and she had proved to have quite extraordinary capabilities that few would have expected in a mere slave. And Lorenzo, she recognized, was no Cosimo.

And it was not just personal relationships that they might have to answer for. Lorenzo could have made peace with Pope Sixtus had he wanted to. It was pride that stopped him. And as a result money had been wasted, homes destroyed, lives lost. The behaviour of princes. Why did it appear so disappointing when viewed with hindsight?

The sacking of Volterra had hardly been his finest hour, either. She had avoided talking about that, knowing, even before the monk's influence changed her perspective, that she had been ashamed of the whole episode. Lorenzo had used false information to pretend that their new alum mine was a threat to Mother Church and its alum monopoly. But the reality had been different. It had been imports of Turkish alum that had spoiled the price and it was not the church but the Medici Bank, with great unsold stocks of the stuff in its warehouses in Bruges, who had stood to lose the money.

Sacking Volterra had been unjustified – a petulant response to people made rebellious by circumstances. And building that great castle with its garrison? Surely that will simply breed resentment? You can't win the hearts and minds of men with soldiers. Not in the end. An occupying force will always be resented, even if they themselves believe they have right on their side. The bitter truth was that Lorenzo had misused power. And the people knew he had.

The behaviour of princes. In victory, they say, you have to be magnanimous. It is a sign, they say, of a great prince. But unlike his father, Lorenzo had shown no mercy after the Pazzi conspiracy. What Francesco Pazzi had done had been wrong, but hounding the whole of the Pazzi family into extinction could really not have been justified. Women and children had suffered, innocent men too. Just because their name was Pazzi. *I know parentado means that families stick together*, she told herself, *but some of these people had done nothing.*

The behaviour of princes! What Lorenzo had been doing for the last few years was hardly something to brag about. Yes she had told him to avoid the trap Cosimo had fallen into. Make the people pay, she had said. But there were ways and ways. She knew that the old way was unsustainable, but already-rich men living off the fat of the land, incurring vast expenses only to lay the bills at the feet of the state, and then authorize the payment themselves, that too was wrong, and equally unsustainable.

Perhaps it would have been different if the bank had still thrived as it had in Giovanni Benci's time? But the truth was they had let it go. Lost control of it. Left the branches in the hands of unsuitable, insufficiently-qualified people, people who were unsupervised, with insufficient regulation or leadership, and in an environment whose very rules motivated them to act irresponsibly.

Whose fault and responsibility had that been? In recent years, her son's. And who had advised him? To a large extent, she had. She knew in her heart-of-hearts that she had acted petulantly. Maliciously. That was the truth of it. She had never forgiven Cosimo for marrying her to Piero. But how else could she get back at him? Only by attacking the one thing he held most dear: the bank. And when Cosimo had lost Benci and had been left on his own, old and not what he had been, and began making mistakes, she had seen her opportunity and she had acted. It hadn't been difficult, she had simply let it happen.

Even before Lorenzo came to power, she had been selfish and angry. Even then, she had seen Francesco Sassetti mismanaging the bank and Giovanni presiding over the decay. And what had she done? She had let it happen. She had stood by and watched it happen and taken pleasure in allocating blame. Malice. It was a sin. An unforgivable sin.

And then, of course, there was the biggest lie of all. Had that been an act of petulance? In part, yes. An act of defiance? Certainly. An act of duplicity? Of course, in the greatest possible way. But it had also been an act of complicity. And both of Cosimo's sons had been complicit with her. It was the one secret, surely, that she could not tell the young monk.

Just desserts, you might say, for wasn't it she who had been complicit with their father, conspired with him and with Maddalena – albeit after their deaths, to defraud the bank and in that respect, to defraud Piero and Giovanni and their partner-cousin, Pierfrancesco, who although he did nothing, still owned fifty percent of the bank? But they had been cheated out of the gold Cosimo had hidden for Lorenzo. That was the truth. And she had played her part in it.

So in the end, she had cheated them all: Cosimo, Piero, Giovanni, Pierfran cesco – all except her beloved sons, Lorenzo and Giuliano. And even then, if you were completely honest with yourself, in making Lorenzo what he had become she had perhaps been partially responsible for causing Giuliano's terrible death.

What an indictment!

And now Savonarola was sitting there, waiting for her confession, and already, the all-seeing God had heard her preparing for it. Even now, he was, perhaps, waiting to see what she told the young monk and what, at her last and final opportunity, she decided to hold back. She felt a sudden shiver of apprehension pass through her, as someone who has just sensed she is being watched. She took a deep breath. The moment had come and already she had gone too far. There was no escape now.

She was aware she had been pacing up and down, not speaking, and for a moment she felt the need to explain. But there was nothing left to explain. The truth was clear. She had declared this to be her confession and in so doing she had unlocked the door of her own waiting prison cell. There was no longer a way to turn back. Now she must enter it.

As she faced that reality and made her decision, she felt her mood change. She took three deep breaths. Feeling calmer than she had for days, she walked to the chair, stroked its back with her hand, then turned to face him and, with a sudden and decisive action, sat down.

'My purpose today is to review and summarize my confession. But as you recognize clearly, my whole story over these recent weeks has also formed part of my confession. Every word of what I have told you is privileged. I shall not return to the city until the heat of summer is over, and I do not expect to live for another year thereafter. So you may not see me again. If you do, please make no reference to these conversations.'

She sat upright and lifted her chin. She was no longer speaking to a young monk from Ferrara, now she was speaking to God. 'Now I seek redemption for the many sins I have committed.

'With my father-in-law I entered into a fraudulent transaction, to remove money from the bank and to make it secretly available to my son, Lorenzo.

'With my husband I neglected the Medici bank and in the process neglected its depositors, its clients and its employees. My husband did not have the capability to run the bank competently, but I did have the knowledge and from behind him I could have brought it back to success. But I did not. I allowed it to fail.

'When my son inherited the opportunity to save the bank, in the form of the great sum Cosimo had put aside for him, I led him to reject that opportunity and instead I told him to use the money in support of his greater aim, to become a great prince.

'With my son Lorenzo I have committed many further sins.'

Suddenly overcome by the magnitude of what she was about to say, she fell to her knees, and as she did so, the words started to spill out and once they started, she couldn't stop them. They kept on flowing.

'I confess that I have given birth to an ogre, a tyrant, a sadist, a monster. But now it is too late. If I am to prevent the collapse of the whole government of the city, which has become dependent upon him, I have to continue to support him, and to pray for his soul as well as my own.

'Our sins are many. Together we neglected the bank, defrauded the bank, defrauding the cousins of their bags of gold, their inheritance from Pier Francesco.

'When the people of Volterra rose up against his unwillingness to return the alum mines to them, I supported my son as, with inappropriate and excessive violence, he sacked the city, put down the people and cowed them into submission by building a great citadel in the heart of their ancient city.

'I also allowed my son to commit revengeful dishonouring of many noble families, particularly the Pazzi, with vindictive pursuit of their families, until they feared for their very lives.

'Together, we are guilty of the destruction of trust and respect, throughout the city, to be replaced by fear. We are guilty of bringing the Republic of Florence into unnecessary war, through pride, through deceitful misuse of the people, through the dissemination of false information and of the enslavement of the republic to the Dukedom of Milan, a treasonable act in the law of the Florentine republic.'

'For these many sins, I ask forgiveness.'

For a moment she considered ending it there, but could she? Surely it was too late? Already God had seen her make her list and if she did not read them all out, she would have compounded the sin.

But yet? Antonio's warning came back to her. *This is not a man to be trusted.*

Could she tell him? Dare she tell him? How could she find the words to describe such an event?

192

~

CAREGGI
16th April 1444

Lucrezia is in Careggi. She is seventeen years old and still reeling from the shock of being told, three days ago, that she will marry Piero. In six weeks she will be married. She has been brought to Careggi by her beloved Giovanni, Piero's brother, to talk about the marriage. She assumes his role is to talk her round. But now this. Nothing prepared her for this.

'Please don't look at me like that, Lucrezia.'

She is finding it hard to speak. Even – perhaps especially, to the man she loves. The man she has loved for perhaps half her life. 'I ... I feel doubly deceived, Giovanni. Deceived by my husband-to-be, even before I am due to marry him, and at the same time, deceived by you – the one love I have had in my life. How can you both do this to me?'

He flaps his hands helplessly. 'What can I say? I admit I have fathered a child with this woman. No, I don't love her but she made herself available to me and she was ...'

'Attractive? You lusted after her? Despite all your soft words to me you were lusting after another woman?'

'It was nothing. She was ... available. That's all. '

'So you bed any woman who is available? Giovanni! How can you sink so low? Do you not realize how such actions diminish me? Me who loves you?'

The hang-dog expression and flapping hands show he has no excuses. She knows he knows her too well to attempt to divert her anger with clever speeches. 'I cannot excuse myself. What is done is done. And I am not, even if I would wish to be with all my heart, betrothed to you.'

That's one point she has to accept. The truth is, she has no hold over him now and he has no obligations to her. 'But why Piero? Why should he pretend to be the father, when he is about to marry me? Why does he humiliate me that way?'

'As I told you, because there is a very good chance I will be made a cardinal. And that will benefit the whole family. If I were to acknowledge a child now, my chances would be ruined. So generously, in my interests and for the sake of the family, Piero has agreed to tell the world the child is his. And by doing so before your marriage, he sought to avoid embarrassment to you. The child and the events that created it pre-date your announcement.'

He gives her the Giovanni special look – the puppy dog embarrassed 'please help me' grin. 'Please understand. Please? We could delay the announcement until after your marriage, if you prefer?'

Exhausted, she nods. She can never beat Giovanni. He always talks her round. But she won't give up completely. 'Perhaps that might be better. But do we have to do everything for the family?'

His head tips from side to side. 'It's not just for the family. Our agreement, the agreement Piero and I have come to, has benefits for you and for me too. And, in truth, for him.'

She frowns. 'Why? How? In what way?'

He takes her hand. 'In the interests of *parentado*, Cosimo has chosen to marry you to Piero. But, and this is difficult to tell you … He can never give you children. Piero is impotent. He can't even – you know – do it.'

'How do you know?'

'Oh come on. Boys – brothers – we talk about such things.'

'You mean I won't have to …? With Piero?'

'Exactly. Not only won't have to, but from what I know, couldn't even if you wanted to.'

She gasps, although whether with shock or relief she is not sure. The prospect of making love with Piero had been a part of the nightmare. 'So I will never have children?' He pulls an awkward face but doesn't reply. 'And if you are to be a celibate cardinal, the Medici male line will end here?'

Giovanni has his puppy face on again. 'Well, I didn't exactly say that, did I?'

'She shakes her head. This is all beyond understanding. 'What then?'

'Listen. As head of the family, Piero needs sons, as you say, to continue the line. But as he has admitted, he cannot father

194

children on you. So …'

'So?' She can almost but not quite guess what's coming. After Giovanni's last revelation, anything's possible.

'Well, as the child Maria shows, I can. So Piero and I have come to an agreement. What you might call a reciprocal agreement. That you and I will make children and that he as your husband and head of the household will publicly accept them as his own.'

She stares at him. She thought she understood the Medici. But this? She is speechless.

Giovanni smiles. 'Neat eh?'

'Neat? Is that what you call it? Almost incestuous adultery and you call it *neat*?'

'Almost incestuous. But not actually. And anyway, nobody need know. Piero gets his children and you and I are, to all intents and purposes, married.' He stands back and looks at her.

She blows her nose. 'But it's sinful.'

'It's not. Not really. Not if we all agree. It's pragmatic. It works. It's what you and I have always wanted.' The head tips from side to side once again. 'Well, almost.' He waits, looking at her as she thinks. 'If after a little time you both feel it's wrong and sinful, you could always get a dispensation from the pope. On the grounds of impotence. It's preferable to an annulment. I'm sure he'd agree.' He takes hold of her elbow. 'Put it this way. It's better than being properly married to Piero isn't it?'

It takes her some time to agree. But she does. And in the end and by the time the shock and surprise have worn off, not all that reluctantly.

~

Lucrezia realized she was biting her lip. She glanced at Savonarola's face, trying to visualize herself looking up, trying to explain.

You see there was the possibility – indeed a strong possibility – that Giovanni would be made a cardinal, and then this child, Maria, came along. The problem was, the mother was a noblewoman and related to the pope. It was too big a risk. So Piero agreed to declare the girl as his own and to promise to look after her as a Medici. He told me the truth at the time and I, shortly to marry him, and wishing to please, and still loving Giovanni and willing to do anything for him, agreed to bring her up as my own.

He might believe that.

It was only when he brought the matter up in the context of the pope's dispensation, that I fully realized what my husband and his brother were telling me, that he knew he could not give me a child but that they believed his brother Giovanni could. Not only that, but in the interests of the family, they were both willing to be complicit in the deception. And it worked. Lorenzo was Giovanni's son. And so was Giuliano. And so were the girls – all of them, although of course, Maria was not mine.

It was flimsy. Riddled with risks when you were talking to a priest. And a zealot priest at that.

It makes no difference. Lorenzo is a true Medici, of the same line and identical grandparents. And I am his true mother.

He wouldn't swallow that, she was sure. It made no difference. She would have to do better than that. And then there was Piero's position to consider. She couldn't put that at risk. Suppose the monk began telling everyone?

Only Lorenzo and I and Giovanni knew the certainty of this. I never told Piero to his face that Lorenzo was not his, and he was careful never to ask me. But of course he knew. It could not possibly have been otherwise

She closed her eyes and heard her own words. How would they sound? How would he respond to them? Silently she tried to rehearse them.

And now, I must confess to one greater sin. With my brother-in-law I committed adultery. In my defence, I shall say that it was with the agreement of my husband, who knew he was unable to give me children. It began when we applied to the pope for a plenaria remissio. Piero told me he had sinned in saying that Maria was his.

Dare she say it? She would have to accompany this confession, more than any of the others, with a strict warning.

Now you share this information under the privilege of the confessional. On sufferance of excommunication and of death. For make no mistake, if ever word of this gets out, Lorenzo will know the source and he will take terrible revenge.

But would it work? Could he be trusted?

She opened her eyes and looked at Savonarola, her mind fighting against itself.

He was looking at her now, with an intensity that made her feel uncomfortable. What did Antonio say? *In the name of religious penance, he almost tortured the young novices.*

There was something wrong with that look, that stillness, that degree of concentration. She felt herself swallow, throat dry, afraid of him.

And then, like a great lizard, his tongue came out and he licked his lips.

This is not a man to be trusted.

She looked at Savonarola and she knew. She couldn't do it.

'This is my confession of the sins I have committed. For these, my many sins, I ask forgiveness.'

Drained of all emotion, she looked at him for a reaction. For some time he sat, absorbing all that she had said. And, perhaps, also, all that he sensed she hadn't said. Even now she knew he was willing her to say more.

She dared not say more. She could not say more. She must end it now.

'Tell me what I must do to save my soul?'

Now the moment had come she was afraid, and she was finding his silence intolerable. That lick of the lips, she had felt as if she was waiting to be devoured. Had she said too much over the weeks? Could he be trusted? The truth was, she didn't know.

He licked his lips again and this time he swallowed hard.

And in that instant, she knew he had accepted that he had just lost.

Appearing beaten, he gave his pronouncement. 'These are indeed many and great sins. I shall have to consider my reply. I will send you my judgement in writing, once I have had time to consider the matter more fully. In the meantime, try to counsel your son to mend his ways, continue in your religious writings and give generously to the poor.'

Epilogue

Early the following morning, Girolamo Savonarola left the Bagno à Morba and walked away, alone.

He followed the narrow lane to the main mountain road, turned right and began to climb up towards the pass, toward Montecerboli, on to Montecastelli, past Monteguidi, through Càsole d'Elsa, and then down the long slope to Colle di Val d'Elsa. From there he would follow the river past Poggio Imperiale before he began the second long climb over the hills to Tavarnelle and then finally down again to Florence, and his future.

He was grim-faced. His sandals were badly worn and he was not sure they would last the long walk. The mist he could see ahead of him would, he knew, soon soak through the rough material of his cassock and his shirt and hair shirt beneath. Before the day was out, the blood from his iron belt would surely be running down his legs, as had happened many times before. And when that happened, passers-by would look at him and start to consider whether he was an escaped criminal, or just, as many had thought in the past, another lunatic monk.

But none of those matters was the reason for his grim face. That was caused by the two questions, questions that niggled away at him as he began to climb.

The first was how to use the knowledge he had gained at the Bagno à Morba in God's name?

Now, he felt, he was starting to understand the city he was returning to. Such deceits and vanities. Burning was the only answer. But how could he bring this about? It would need long and careful thought, and slow and careful action. It might take him years. But at least he knew who to talk to now. And what questions to ask them. And which of their answers to believe.

There was no rush. God was not in any hurry.

But at that moment, as he started to climb into the barren hills, the question that was really troubling him was the second one. How could he get all the way to the Monastery of San Marco in Florence without his secret being discovered?

His secret was a burden, both physically and mentally. If discovered, he would not last one day in front of Lorenzo. The very thought of it made his throat go dry. For in his leather satchel, beside his bible, wrapped in his now-bulging breviary and surrounded by his spare shirt, were pages and pages of detailed notes, each in his tiny spidery handwriting. Between them, they recorded everything that Mona Lucrezia had said.

Author's Note

The rapid rise and the equally rapid collapse of the Medici Bank (which was effectively all over in less than a hundred years) is a remarkable story – not least because there are so many parallels with the banking crisis of the present period.

For those who wish to understand these issues in detail, I recommend Tim Parks' *Medici Money* for an outstanding and clearly written overview and Raymond de Roover's *The Rise and Decline of the Medici Bank 1397-1494* for a detailed textbook analysis.

What I have tried to do in the series *The House of Medici* is to tell the story from a human point of view. What was it like to live through these great events, to face the great opportunities offered to successive Medici sons but also to manage the problems that regularly occurred in a rapidly changing world and to suffer the disappointments when people let you down?

And in all of this, to try to answer the question: 'How did it all go so disastrously wrong?'

In the first book in the series, *The House of Medici – Inheritance of Power*, we saw how Cosimo de' Medici faithfully passed on the rules given to him by his father, but at the same time allowed his own actions to break those rules more often than they reflected them.

First, the new partnership structure no longer protected the family from losses incurred within the widely spread branches. Second, Cosimo's choice of managers broke all his father's rules of promoting the best and not the family. Third, the new partnership agreements with the branches motivated the branch managers to act foolhardily and in their own local interests. And fourth, slippage in maintaining the bank's originally strict systems of annual audit meant that the centre did not recognize problems until it was far too late.

It was this slippery slope that Piero inherited.

Unfortunately it was the same with politics. Cosimo had always presented the Medici as commoners, members of the *popolani*, but his true intentions were visible to those who took the trouble to put aside his words and instead to observe his deeds. He had married Contessina Bardi, the daughter of a count, and later he married his elder son Piero to Lucrezia Tornabuoni.

It turned out to be one of his greatest mistakes, as this second book, *The House of Medici – Seeds of Decline* , tries to show.

Cosimo tried to protect the family's future from the weakness he could see all too plainly in Piero. First, he tried putting his second son Giovanni in charge of the bank. Second, he hid a fortune – *Lorenzo's Gold*, 200,000 Florins (£24 million in today's money) – deep beneath a convent in order to give his grandson the opportunity to salvage something from the mess he knew Piero would inevitably leave behind. And finally, in a feeble attempt to prop up his son's weaknesses, he forced Lucrezia Tornabuoni to marry Piero.

Lucrezia was one of the outstanding women of her age, not only a poet but a successful businesswoman in her own right, owning shops and a hotel in Pisa and the medicinal baths at Bagno à Morba, south of Volterra, which she personally redeveloped into a thriving business. Uncomfortably for both of them, she was considerably brighter and more able than Piero. Not only that, but (as Cosimo was fully aware) she was in love with his younger brother – her childhood hero Giovanni.

What Cosimo was not to know was that in her resentment over her marriage, Lucrezia would bring up her precocious son Lorenzo in direct opposition to the Medici Creed. She could see through both facades. She understood partnership agreements, selection and recruitment of managers, contracts, motivation and financial controls. It was obvious to her that the bank was on the slide.

She also understood that the Florentine Republic was an unsustainable pretence, a dream that had never really existed as the mirror of classical democracy that the priors told each other they were presiding over. The system of checks and balances that they had built into the rules two hundred years before had always acted as a constraint on effective government to the point of stifling good administration. And while they told themselves that the city state maintained itself financially, proudly refusing to allow any one individual to bear the burden of expenditure for fear he should become 'a Great Prince', the truth was that during his lifetime Cosimo had spent 660,000 Florins (today worth £75 million) on great municipal projects and propping up the city's finances, and secretly they all knew it.

Lucrezia could see that, generous a gift as *Lorenzo's Gold* might be, the task Cosimo was implicitly asking his grandson to achieve with it was an impossible one. Instead she used all her power openly to make him *Lorenzo the Magnificent*, a Great Prince; one who forced through change and who, by blurring the boundaries between personal and state expenditure, progressively pushed the burden back where it belonged. Unfortunately, much of that blurring had questionable legality. And at the same time, between them, they were letting the family bank go to the dogs.

Yet in addition to all her temporal abilities, Lucrezia was also a very devout woman. As she approached the end of her life she began to worry about the legality – and perhaps as important – the morality of what she had led Lorenzo to become. She had acted in what she thought was the appropriate manner – guiding her son to pursue reality not dreams, but in the process, what had she created? How would she finally be remembered? What would be her epitaph when finally her life was over?

And then there was her son. Lorenzo the Magnificent himself. What would be the outcome of his life after she was gone? How would he be remembered? As a great leader, who guided Florence through adversity to eventual triumph? Or as a domineering ogre who would stop at nothing to get his own way? Would Lorenzo regret his actions as he too approached the end of his life? And would he, in those dying days, thank her for what she had led him toward?

Only time would tell. But that, as they say, is another story; a story told by *The House of Medici – Decline and Fall*.